A Birmingham Family Christmas
(Brazen Brides Series, Book 5)

When spinster Annabelle Lippencott is invited
by her cousin, Emma Birmingham, to spend
Christmas with the extended Birmingham
Family, little does she expect to find Spencer
Woodruff, the man who broke her heart eleven
years earlier.

With His Ring *(Brides of Bath, Book 2)*
"Cheryl Bolen does it again! There is laughter, and the interaction of the characters pulls you right into the book. I look forward to the next in this series." – *RT Book Reviews*

The Bride's Secret *(Brides of Bath, Book 3)*
*(*originally titled *A Fallen Woman)*
"What we all want from a love story...Don't miss it!"
– *In Print*

To Take This Lord *(Brides of Bath, Book 4)*
*(*originally titled *An Improper Proposal)*
"Bolen does a wonderful job building simmering sexual tension between her opinionated, outspoken heroine and deliciously tortured, conflicted hero." – *Booklist of the American Library Association*

My Lord Wicked
Winner, International Digital Award for Best Historical Novel of 2011.

With His Lady's Assistance *(Regent Mysteries, Book 1)*
"A delightful Regency romance with a clever and personable heroine matched with a humble, but intelligent hero. The mystery is nicely done, the romance is enchanting and the secondary characters are enjoyable." – *RT Book Reviews*

Finalist for International Digital Award for Best Historical Novel of 2011.

A Duke Deceived
"*A Duke Deceived* is a gem. If you're a Georgette Heyer fan, if you enjoy the Regency period, if you like a genuinely sensuous love story, pick up this first novel by Cheryl Bolen."
– *Happily Ever After*

Books by Cheryl Bolen

Regency Romance

Brazen Brides Series
   Counterfeit Countess (Book 1)
   His Golden Ring (Book 2)
   Oh What A (Wedding) Night (Book 3)
   Miss Hastings' Excellent London Adventure
      (Book 4)
   A Birmingham Family Christmas (Book 5)

House of Haverstock Series
   Lady by Chance (Book 1)
   Duchess by Mistake (Book2)
   Countess by Coincidence (Book 3)
   Ex-Spinster by Christmas (Book 4)

The Brides of Bath Series:
   The Bride Wore Blue (Book 1)
   With His Ring (Book 2)
   The Bride's Secret (Book 3)
   To Take This Lord (Book 4)
   Love in the Library (Book 5)
   A Christmas in Bath (Book 6)

The Regent Mysteries Series:
   With His Lady's Assistance (Book 1)
   A Most Discreet Inquiry (Book 2)
   The Theft Before Christmas (Book 3)
   An Egyptian Affair (Book 4)

The Earl's Bargain
My Lord Wicked
His Lordship's Vow

A Duke Deceived

Novellas:
Christmas Brides (3 Regency Novellas)
Only You

Inspirational Regency Romance
Marriage of Inconvenience

Romantic Suspense
Texas Heroines in Peril Series:
    Protecting Britannia
    Capitol Offense
    A Cry in the Night
    Murder at Veranda House

Falling for Frederick

American Historical Romance
*A Summer to Remember (*3 American Historical Romances)

World War II Romance
It Had to be You

A BIRMINGHAM FAMILY CHRISTMAS

(Brazen Brides Series, Book 5)

CHERYL BOLEN

Brazen Brides Family Tree

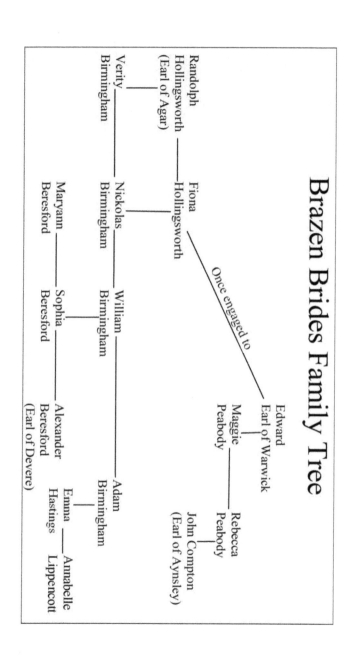

$\mathcal{C}$hapter 1

"I have accepted that I'm an old maid and shall never attract a husband." Miss Annabelle Lippincott faced her much-younger cousin and shrugged. One might expect Annabelle to be jealous of Emma, who'd had the stupendous good fortune to have recently married the most sought-after bachelor in the kingdom. Adam Birmingham was not only vastly wealthy, but he was possessed of fine looks and appeared to be devoted to dear little Emma.

But Annabelle could never be jealous of her cousin. The confirmed spinster held firmly to the belief that happiness was a carefully measured commodity not indiscriminately bestowed. In Annabelle's own case, all her happiness had been spent in the first half of her privileged life. She had grown up in the mansion of her baronet grandfather and was thoroughly doted upon by her father who credited her with far more beauty and accomplishments than she actually possessed. Now into the second half of her life, she was resigned to a loveless existence.

Poor Emma, on the other hand, had endured a sad childhood as the orphan ward of a stern, exceedingly ancient maiden aunt. Now Emma collected her portion of blissful happiness.

Emma's eyes narrowed as she regarded her elder cousin and put hands to her hips. "That's the most foolish thing I've ever heard you say!

You're acting as if your life is over, and you are but eight-and-twenty."

"I've been on the shelf so long several new waves of debutantes have come and gone--and most of them fared far better than I." Annabelle's lashes lowered. Better that than seeing pity in Emma's eyes.

"Can you honestly tell me you received no offers during your Season?"

"I will own that my dowry no doubt attracted several suitors, but . . . the ones who offered for me were the ones who did not suit me, and the only one who suited chose not to . . . to officially offer for me."

"I was quite young at the time, but I recall that you were very melancholy when you returned to Lower Barrington following your London Season. I was convinced you'd come home with a broken heart." Emma came closer, touched Annabelle's forearm, and spoke softly. "Was I correct?"

All these years later the very memory of Spencer Woodruff had the power to accelerate Annabelle's heartbeat and summon tears she was determined not to spill. She had believed him when he said he would ask her father for permission to marry her. Every day those first two years she had looked for him. Every day her father had assured her he'd heard not a word from Mr. Woodruff. Every night she had wept for him in the privacy of her bedchamber.

Annabelle nodded. "I did fancy myself in love."

"Did he not return your regard?"

Annabelle vividly remembered that night beneath the stars at Vauxhall Gardens when he'd taken her hand in his. *I have nothing to offer you but my heart, but if you would do me the goodness of becoming my wife, I will spend the rest of my life trying to make myself worthy of you."*

Recalling the very timbre of his voice, she sighed and faced Emma. "He said he did. He led me to believe he was as strongly attracted to me as I was to him." She shook her head. "I've asked myself thousands of times *why him*? He was neither titled nor wealthy, but the first time he spoke to me I believed he was The One with whom I would spend the rest of my life. No one before or since has ever affected me so profoundly."

"Oh, my dear Annabelle. I am very sorry, but that beastly man was certainly not worthy of you!"

"He wasn't beastly. He was an honorable man. I know it."

"I will own, you have always been possessed of sound judgment. You're the most mature, level-headed person I've ever known. Even when you were a child. Perhaps the man who captured your ardor may have been beset by some tragedy that prevented him from speaking to your father?"

"I've spent the past eleven years asking myself the same question."

"You need to know--if for nothing else than to restore your faith in men."

"While Papa lived, I could never write to a gentleman. Now so many years have passed I wouldn't know how to go about trying to learn what became of him."

"After Christmas, Adam and I will help you."

Annabelle's gaze flicked to the clock upon the mantel in her bedchamber, or rather the bedchamber where she slept at Emma's impressive new home. It was noon. They were to leave for the country in less than an hour. "Are you certain Mr. Nicholas Birmingham won't mind me intruding on the family's Christmas at Camden Hall?"

"You goose! You *are* family! Even though I'm so recent an addition to the Birminghams they make me feel as if I were a sister of the blood. They will all conspire to make you feel a part of this big, caring clan."

If only. As an only child, Annabelle had always longed for siblings. Emma was her closest relation, and there were eight years between them. "I know there are three Birmingham brothers: Adam, Nicholas and William." She'd heard of the family's vast wealth long before her cousin had ever come to London and snared one of them. "But are there any sisters?"

Emma nodded. "One. Verity. You'll have the pleasure of meeting her, too. She'll be making the trip from Windmere Abbey in Yorkshire."

Annabelle's eyes widened. "Is Windmere Abbey not the home of the Earls of Agar?"

"Indeed. Verity *is* Lady Agar, and she's now the mother of the future Lord Agar who is the most beautiful baby boy ever in existence."

Annabelle had not expected to be mingling with *real* nobility. "Had I known we'd be enjoying intercourse with the aristocracy I would have brought my best gowns." Then she realized it had been so long since she'd had occasion to wear one, she had likely outgrown them.

"Don't give it another thought. None of the ladies are slaves to fashion, nor are they judgmental. They are incredibly kind."

"You cannot mean there is more than one titled lady coming?"

"Oh, yes. Both of Adam's brothers married earl's daughters. Lady Sophia's married to William

Birmingham, the youngest brother. She's the daughter of the Earl of Devere, and Nick's wife is Lady Fiona, whose brother is Lord Agar."

Annabelle sighed. "I would wager all those ladies are beautiful." *Unlike me.* Annabelle was well aware that as she had aged, she'd gotten fat-- not fat like those hideous caricatures of Lady Hamilton, but definitely plump. Another reason she would never attract a husband.

"Yes, they are beautiful, and I know what you must be thinking. *How did a little country mouse like the former Emma Hastings ever capture the best prize on the Marriage Mart?*"

"I most certainly was not!" Though, truth be told, that is exactly what Annabelle had been thinking. Emma was bereft of beauty and fortune. At least, she had not been a beauty when she'd left Upper Barrington for London months earlier. But now, with the clothing and hair dressing her husband's fortune could procure, Emma had been transformed into something quite lovely. Annabelle could not help but admire Adam Birmingham for recognizing Emma's wonderful qualities. "Mr. Adam Birmingham is very fortunate to have won your hand in marriage." In this praise, Miss Annabelle Lippincott was most sincere.

"I am well aware of my blessings, and now my fondest wish is for you to find such bliss." Emma pressed her hands to her cousin's. "I couldn't bear to think of you all alone at Christmas. Now that your father's gone, you must live with us. We are your family."

Annabelle was almost overcome with emotion. Amongst all Emma's blessings and constant activities with her new family, she worried about her cousin. "I confess I was happy to receive your invitation. I'm looking forward to going to Camden Hall."

* * *

Spencer's employer, standing near the door and wrapping a muffler around his neck, eyed him. "Will you be spending Christmas with your sister's family?" Adam Birmingham asked.

Spencer Woodruff set down his pen and shook his head. "No. She's gone to Shropshire to be with her husband's family."

"A pity Shropshire's so beastly far away."

"Indeed. Those of us who must work for a living can't neglect our duties for that many days." Spencer could speak frankly to Adam for even though he was one of the wealthiest men in England, Adam Birmingham almost never missed a day at his bank. The only reason he was able to celebrate the Yule with his family was the close proximity to London of Nicholas Birmingham's estate, where the family gathered every Christmas.

"It's also a pity you don't have a wife," Adam added.

Adam Birmingham could also speak freely to Spencer. Despite the disparity in their wealth, the two had become fast friends at Cambridge. Both had been outsiders, Adam because his crass father had pulled himself up from the lower classes, and Spencer because he was a penniless scholarship student.

When Spencer left school he accepted a position as Adam's clerk and in the ensuing years had risen to become vice president of the powerful Birmingham Bank. "I won't be marrying. I learned in a most cruel fashion that women are not truthful."

"I won't listen to you maligning women. I've the good fortune to have married an exceedingly truthful woman who has made me the happiest man in the kingdom."

Spencer smiled. "I'm very happy for you."

Adam moved to him and slapped him on the back. "I won't hear of you spending Christmas alone in London. You must come to Camden Hall."

Spencer was also close to Nicholas Birmingham and had been to the impressive Camden Hall once before. "I shouldn't like to intrude on your family gathering."

"But you're like family. Nick certainly thinks so, and Emma has also grown very fond of you. Besides, it won't all be family. Well, Birmingham family. Emma's cousin's coming. She lost her father earlier this year, and Emma wouldn't allow her to be alone--just as I won't allow you to be alone at Christmas. You'll come to Camden. That's an order." Adam grabbed his beaver and walking stick, strode to the door, then turned back. "You've worked enough today, Pythagoras."

Spencer wondered if old school chums would ever stop referring to him by the name they'd dubbed him because of his prowess in mathematics.

Seconds after the door closed, Adam came back. "There will be a place for you at Camden's dinner table tonight. We eat at five."

Spencer nodded. Christmas at Camden Hall sounded much more inviting than eating mutton at his bachelor quarters in Bloomsbury.

* * *

Nick was worried about his mother and Verity. Mama was to have opened Great Acres last week in preparation for Christmas, but they still hadn't arrived from Verity's house in Yorkshire. The courier he'd sent to Great Acres early that morning had just informed him that his mother and sister had not yet arrived in Surrey.

Nick had heard that it was snowing in Yorkshire. Had their party--Mama, Verity and Agar, and their babe--been forced to abort their travel and wait out the weather at an inn? Or, worse still, had they been stranded and buried under snow? Nick could not purge his memory of Lord Acer's icy death many years ago. That man had been caught in a brutal snow storm on a secluded country road in Yorkshire.

Nick worried, too, about Verity. Though she had not spoken of it--the proud new mother only spoke of that baby boy of hers--Nick thought her weakened after her lying-in. During that one brief meeting with her whilst he was electioneering in Yorkshire, Nick had been upset by her altered appearance. Her colour was off, and instead of adding girth, she had obviously lost weight.

Was that why they were late arriving? Had her health declined? Good Lord, had she died? Just last week Mr. Holmes had lost his wife two months after she gave birth--something from which she had never recovered. She was but two-and-twenty.

Nick's gut plunged. He could not bear to contemplate losing his cherished only sister.

But perhaps Mama was the one who'd gotten sick. Even though she was a septuagenarian, she had always exhibited remarkably good health.

He wouldn't have a moment's peace until all of his family was home and safe for Christmas.

$\mathcal{C}$hapter 2

Even when Papa was alive, their Christmases were dull occasions. When Annabelle had received the invitation from Emma to come spend her first Christmas without Papa with the Birminghams, she had leapt at the opportunity. The exhilaration of returning to London, the reassurance that Emma was being cherished, the notion of spending Christmas at the eldest Birmingham brother's fine estate, all had lifted her spirits.

Mingling with members of the nobility both awed her and terrified her at the same time. Even though she was the daughter of a baronet, her only previous association with higher ranking aristocrats had been when she was presented to the queen all those years ago, the same time she'd briefly spoken to the titled patronesses at Almack's. Now she would be staying in the same house with the daughters of Lords Agar and Devere.

The latter lady, at the last moment, had joined them for the carriage ride to Surrey, where Nicholas Birmingham's Camden Hall was located."I do hope you'll permit me to ride with you to Camden Hall," Lady Sophia said with a bright smile and shrug to her dainty shoulders. "I'd much rather be with you ladies than be obliged to listen to William and Nick rattling off about their stock exchange."

She climbed onto the carriage seat next to

Annabelle. "I beg that you dispense with formal introductions," she said to Emma. Then she directed a sweet smile at Annabelle. "I declare, Miss Lippincott, I do see a resemblance between you and Emma. It's your nose and something about the mouth." She took Annabelle's hands in hers. "Emma is so fortunate to have you, and we are so fortunate that you're to be joining us for Christmas."

Upon seeing Lady Sophia's radiant dark-haired beauty, Annabelle became glaringly aware of her own advancing age and expanding waistline. Even the dress she wore no longer seemed so smart when compared to the simple elegance of Lady Sophia's rosy velvet frock with matching pelisse. These inadequacies should have rendered Miss Annabelle Lippincott mute, but strangely she was not.

One moment in the gracious lady's company dispelled any shyness Annabelle might have possessed. Lady Sophia was the only person who had ever acknowledged the similarity between the two cousins. Most people only saw that Emma was tiny and Annabelle was . . . not tiny. No one ever saw that the two shared the Lippincott nose.As time went on, the lady directed her comments at Annabelle as if every word emanating from   that lady's mouth was fascinating.

Even though Lady Sophia teased that she did not want to ride with her husband, her comments about him could not disguise her deep affection. "I'm so happy that I will get to spend the next three days with my dear William."Adam and Emma's obvious devotion to one another was equally apparent. The Birmingham brothers' solid marriages were almost enough to restore Annabelle's faith in love. *Almost.* If only Spencer had not betrayed her.

Thinking about Spencer reminded her of the wealthy old brewer her father had wanted her to marry. "Did you know, Emma, that Mr. Marsden died last month?"

"I did not. He was older than your father, was he not?"

"Slightly."

"Much too old for you to marry. I remember when your father took that silly notion into his head that you and Mr. Marsden would suit."

Annabelle shook her head sadly. "Papa only favored him because of his immense fortune."

Emma nodded. "You must own, being mistress of Fleur House would have been lovely--if you didn't have to wed its owner!" She turned to her husband. "There's a great deal of money to be made in brewing."

Adam's brows raised. "*That* Mr. Marsden? He is, er, *was* the wealthiest brewer in England."

As they drove up the long drive to Camden Hall, the last vestiges of daylight illuminated the sprawling Palladian mansion. Its Portland stone looked almost golden in the waning sun. Much larger than the home she'd grown up in, Camden was one of the largest homes in the shire. Annabelle counted thirteen chimneys. "What a lovely house!"

"I wish I could say it's been in our family for generations like your home, Miss Lippincott, or Lady Sophia's," Adam said, "but my brother bought the house from Lord Hartley several years ago. So any praise belongs to the marquess who oversaw the construction. Lord Hartley employed

Robert Adam and Capability Brown, so it is rather an impressive place."

"I love the symmetry of Palladian buildings," Annabelle said.Adam nodded. "Nick likes everything orderly."

Lady Sophia laughed. "Not my William."

"They are vastly different--not just in appearance," Adam said.When the coach came to stop in front of the portico, Adam turned to his wife. "I forgot to tell you Woodruff should be here by dinnertime. I didn't like to think of him being alone in London for Christmas."

Just hearing the name Woodruff sent Annabelle's heartbeat skittering. Of course, this gentleman couldn't be *her* Mr. Woodruff.

Emma eyed Annabelle. "Mr. Woodruff is Adam's most dependable employee. They've known each other since they were at university together. He's now the vice president of the bank."

Adam Birmingham *would* be about the same age as Spencer Woodruff. Annabelle's heartbeat roared. She began to tremble. Her voice was thin when she asked, "Wh-a-a-at university w-w-would that be?" Goodness! What had come over her? She'd never stuttered in her life.

"Cambridge."

The same university Spencer Woodruff had attended.

* * *

Annabelle was astonished when she met Nicholas Birmingham who, along with his delicately fair wife, cordially greeted them. He could be Adam's twin. Both men were taller than average and possessed of very dark hair and eyes. And both were strikingly handsome.As friendly as Nicholas and his wife were, Annabelle was stupefied by the speculation that Spencer Woodruff might be here. Try as she did to direct her attention upon her hosts, her traitorous gaze kept leaping about the chamber, searching for a glimpse of the man she had once loved. She had to remove herself from prying eyes that were sure to detect her trembling.

Her wish was soon granted when she was permitted to follow the housekeeper to her bedchamber on the second floor. Were she not in such turmoil, she would have exclaimed over the room's loveliness. The walls were covered with Damask that was more green than blue but a combination of the two hues, a colour she'd never before seen. It paired brilliantly with the stark white woodwork and touches of gilt. The tester bed was covered in the same colour, in silk.Her French maid, who'd come ahead in the servants' coach, had already unpacked her valise and was there to help her mistress dress for dinner. Tears squirting from her eyes, Annabelle collapsed into her chair in front of the dressing table. "I charge you, Marie, with an impossible task. I wish you to make me look half as pleasing as I looked the night of my come-out."

"Then you must wear the blue to show your eyes. Your eyes, they are excrement."

"I do hope you mean exquisite."

"*Oui!*"

As she often did, Annabelle shook her head. Dear Marie was kind enough, first, not to suggest maidenly white. Annabelle was too long in the tooth for debutante white. And, secondly, her maid had kindly meant to comment on Annabelle's eyes, which had always been her best feature. "The blue, I think, an excellent choice."

"It's been a long time, no, since mademoiselle has cared to have her hair styled? I have seen pictures in the newspapers of the Duchess of Wiggins and have been desirous of fashioning that style for you."

Annabelle pictured the beautiful duchess. "How I wish I could look as lovely as she. Her hair is vastly admired. I should adore such a becoming style."

Fortunately, Marie was a talented hairdresser.

As Annabelle sat morosely staring into her looking glass, she contemplated Adam Birmingham's employee. There was no doubt that Adam Birmingham's Mr. Woodruff was *her* Mr. Woodruff. No matter how shabbily he had treated her, she wanted him to still find her attractive.She was nearly overcome at the prospect of seeing him again. Her heartbeat raced, her breathing was erratic. She cautioned herself not to get too excited because he was still unwed. Whatever had prevented him from asking her father for her hand was more than likely still an impediment.Her insides sank. He might also be repulsed over the changes in her appearance. She was, most regrettably, plump. Fortunately, the high waistlines that were in fashion helped conceal her spreading girth. Unfortunately, the low necklines that were fashionable revealed her enlarged bosom spilling from her bodice.

When Marie finished styling her hair, Annabelle was extraordinarily pleased. Her mousy brown hair, which tended to be too curly, had been swept back with diamond pins and shaped into ringlets. She had not looked so handsome in years.As she descended the stairs, every particle of her body trembled. Even her hand gliding along the banister shook so much her ring clattered against the brass rail. When she reached the drawing room, her trembling subsided--once she assured herself Mr. Woodruff had not arrived. The three Birmingham brothers were present: Nick and Lady Fiona, Adam and Emma, and Lady Sophia with her husband William, who looked nothing like the other two Birmingham brothers. He was much shorter, much more muscular, and much more fair with hair of dark blond. After Lady Sophia presented her husband to Annabelle, Lady Fiona, her delicate hand on a young man's sleeve, came up to Annabelle. "Stephen," she said to the fellow, "I should like to present Miss Annabelle Lippincott to you. She is Emma's cousin."

Nearly a decade Annabelle's junior, the young man was all that was courteous in his greetings to her. He bowed. "It's a pleasure to make your acquaintance, Miss Lippincott."

"Stephen's my youngest brother," Lady Fiona added.Though Lady Fiona was delicately built, Annabelle could see a resemblance. Lord Stephen was neither as fair as Fiona, nor as slightly built, but his eyes were the exact same blue as his sister's, and his hair several shades darker than hers but still blond. Though he wasn't as tall as Nick--few men were--he was several inches taller than Annabelle, who was of average height.

The group moved to the dinner room and were seated according to precedence, which ranked Annabelle, the daughter of a baronet, just under Lady Sophia and their hostess, Lady Fiona. They all took their seats, and Annabelle found herself seated at one side of their host. That was when she noticed the empty place setting beside her. *Spencer Woodruff's.*Had he heard that she was to be here and decided not to come? What had she ever done to destroy his affections?The wine was poured, and Nick offered a toast. "May this be the happiest Christmas ever."Then the door creaked open, and the butler announced, "Mr. Spencer Woodruff."

All eyes--including hers--turned to the newcomer. Her heartbeat thundered. He was just as handsome as he'd been a decade earlier. Perhaps even more handsome. The tall youthful frame from which his clothing had once hung had now filled out most admirably. He still dressed in simple good taste, but it wouldn't have mattered what he wore. Such a manly physique! Such a flawless face! She was powerless to remove her gaze from him. His close-cropped ginger hair framed a square, masculine face. She recalled that when he smiled, dimples pierced those angular cheeks. She could swoon.Then his eyes met hers. He froze.Adam stood. "You know all the ladies here except my wife's cousin. Permit me to introduce you to Miss Lippincott."

Spencer raised a brow and started to say something, then clamped shut his mouth.Annabelle had not risen. She felt as if she should curtsy, but one could hardly do so from a seated position, and it was not a lady's duty to rise when a man entered the chamber. So she sat there, wondering if she should say, "We've already met."Her former suitor took the decision away from her. He bowed. "It's lovely to meet you, Miss Lippincott."

For a moment, she cringed with the most sickening feeling that he had forgotten her. Then she remembered how he'd frozen when he saw her. *He does remember me.*Pretending they had never met, she realized, was easier. No explanations needed. She could be spared the humiliation of everyone knowing about his rejection of her.

Her trembles returned. She was afraid to respond to him for fear her voice would give her away. She attempted to regard him with a steely expression, nodding. "Mr. Woodruff." Those were as many words as she could produce.Then her wine glass slipped from her shaky hands.

Fearing her dress would be soiled, she leapt from her chair as a footman rushed to blot the spreading liquid. Fortunately, her dress was spared, but not her pride. She had never in her life been so clumsy. She had wanted to make a good impression. Now she'd merely made an impression. Everyone at the table--and most especially Spencer--was bound to think her a bungling oaf.

Once her mess was cleaned and order restored, she took her seat. "I do apologize for my massive clumsiness. I cannot think how that happened."

Emma sighed. "I can. I do the same thing with great frequency. I don't know how Adam puts up with me."

Adam smiled across the table at his wife. "Ah, because you're so loveable, my sweet."

Spencer addressed their host. "I, too, must apologize. I beg that you forgive me for my tardiness."

"Nothing to forgive," Nick said. "We've only just entered the chamber. Do have a seat." He indicated the chair next to Annabelle.

* * *

For the last eleven years he'd wondered how he would address the woman who had destroyed his happiness, and when it came down to it, he couldn't even acknowledge her. That is not to say he was unaffected by her. Quite the contrary. All these years he had told himself that he despised her. Yet when he saw her sitting there, it was rather like a wallop to his chest.Most shocking of all, she still bore her maiden name.Though she looked much older, he found her more desirable than she'd been as a debutante. There was a womanly curvature about her he found most alluring. Her hair was the same shade of rich brown, but it seemed more radiant than ever. And it wasn't just because there were diamonds in it. Her complexion was as milky as he remembered, and the pink in her cheeks made her looks angelic.

A pity she was not.She was in want of a heart. Miss Annabelle Lippincott had promised to wed him, but when he met with her father to ask for her hand, he'd been informed she'd had decided to marry another. She hadn't even bothered to tell him face to face.

Her eyes, still such a brilliant blue, had regarded him icily. That one glare told him all he needed to know. There had been times in the past decade when he had made excuses for her abrupt betrayal, but any flickering hopes he'd ever had of winning back her affections were instantly snuffed tonight.

As soon as he'd sat beside her, he'd drawn in her sweet lavender scent and was swamped with the powerful memories it evoked. With a hitch to his breath, he recalled the first time her fragrant lavender had destroyed his reserve. It was when they waltzed at the Richardsons' ball and he knew when his hand rested at her waist that he wanted to spend his life with the sweet-smelling girl.

More somberly, he recalled the last time he'd been aware of her scent that night at Vauxhall, the night she told him she loved him and wanted to marry him. *The lying she-devil.*She passed him the French sauce, and their hands briefly touched. He should have recoiled, but he was too affected by her to do so. Instead his gaze met hers. Those blasted eyes of hers had always sent his pulses thumping.The pity of it was, in all these years nothing had changed. Year after year he had loathed her, and after one moment in her presence he felt like a wet youth just down from Cambridge.

But he wasn't a wet youth. He was a man of two-and-thirty years. He had learned the painful lesson that women were not to be trusted. And he wasn't about to fall back under this woman's spell.Even if she wanted him. Which she most certainly did not. She didn't eleven years ago, and she didn't now. In fact, she had disliked him so much she would rather be a spinster than plight her life to his. He was madder than ever. More hurt than ever.

He needed to get his mind off the woman who sat beside him. He helped himself to turbot, silently passed the plate to her, then looked around the table. "I thought Lady Agar was coming for Christmas."

"Verity will be here," Nick said. There was something in his voice that lacked his usual confidence.

His wife's brows lowered. "I thought they were supposed to have come a week or two ago."

Nick nodded. "They were. I suspect the snow may have delayed them."

Lady Fiona sighed. "I hated to mention it when we briefly saw her during the electioneering, but I did not think she looked robust. I do hope her lying-in did not diminish her good health."

"I, too, thought she looked poorly," Adam said, "but I didn't want to alarm anyone."

"If she were doing poorly," Lady Fiona said, "my brother would not have allowed her to travel to meet us. You know how totally devoted he is to her."

"I hope you're right." Nick's voice was again uncharacteristically weak.

Spencer felt a change of conversation was needed. He eyed Lady Fiona. "Is little Emmie looking forward to Christmas?"

She smiled. "She is indeed. We're busy putting together baskets to give to the cottagers. She loves to help me deliver them and see the children's happy faces."

"Christmas is a somber affair without children," he said. "I shall enjoy being here with all of you, and being with Emmie will help make up for not seeing my niece and nephew at Christmas."

A querying look crossed Emma's face. "Does your sister not live in London?" Spencer nodded. "But they are spending Christmas in Shropshire with her in-laws."

"Well, we are very happy to have you," Emma Birmingham said. Then she eyed Annabelle. "And you too, my dear cousin. I hope you never go back to Lower Barrington." Annabelle shrugged. "It's the only place I've ever lived. Do you not miss Upper Barrington?"

Adam's wife shook her head firmly. "I was never happy there." She looked across the table at her husband. "And I am blissfully happy now."

A crooked grin on his face, Adam winked at his wife.

Seeing all these besotted couples made Spencer more aware than ever of what was missing in his life. He'd been deprived of a loving spouse because of this woman seated beside him. It was bad enough that she had lied to him and shredded his heart, but because of her, he could never love another.It wasn't just that he could never again trust a woman. More than anything, he couldn't love again because no other woman possessed those indefinable qualities Annabelle Lippincott possessed; no other woman could ever measure up to her. Even after all these years, he was drawn to her like an opium eater craves his opium.

After dinner and after the gentlemen enjoyed their port, they rejoined the women for games of whist. "Mr. Woodruff, you must be partners with Miss Lippincott," Lady Fiona said.

$\mathcal{C}$hapter 3

"You're very fortunate, Mr. Woodruff, to have my cousin for a partner," Emma said. "Annabelle's most skillful at whist."

"Pray, do not boast on me. Mr. Woodruff is sure to be disappointed if I prove a poor player." All that kept Annabelle from completely falling apart was the comfort of having her cousin and Adam seated on either side. It was difficult enough to pretend she didn't know Spencer. How doubly awkward conversation would have been with a pair she'd only met that day.Spencer eyed her. "I am sure you could never be incompetent, Miss Lippincott."

The intensity of his gaze unruffled her. Her lashes lowered. Before she had peered into his mossy eyes, she had gathered enough composure to plan to say, *"Thank you for your confidence, Mr. Woodruff."* But as soon as she was drawn into the simmering heat of him, she once again became mute.

She knew that her silence made her appear rude. She knew Emma would be disappointed in her. Adam, too. But she felt as if any word issuing from her mouth would sound like quivering, garbled rubbish, and that would draw even more consternation. So she said not a word.

It cut her like a rapier to see the embarrassed look on Spencer's face when she failed to reply.They all took their places at the table. She was happy theirs was placed near the fire, for the drawing room, with its cold stone floors and soaring ceiling, made her shiver. She suspected there was a blue tinge to her exposed shoulders. *Why, oh why, did I ever come?* Her home in Lower Barrington may have been a lonely, quiet place, but it did offer a comforting familiarity. Nothing here at Camden Hall was familiar, and seeing Spencer after all these years was like reopening a gaping, painful wound.

Why have I done this to myself? She was so ashamed. She could tell by the stiffness in Adam Birmingham's countenance that he was displeased with her. Now she knew what it felt like to bite the hand that fed one.Dear Emma attempted to smooth over an awkward situation. "Well now, shall we see if I am right about my cousin? I'll deal."

Spencer was bound to think her hopelessly inept at whist. She could only barely concentrate upon her pasteboards. Would she ever again be able to speak to this man she had thought herself in love with for so very long? Would an easy peace between them ever develop? How was she going to manage being so close to him for the next three days?*I must concentrate on the pasteboards.* Not on Spencer."How lovely that blue dress is on you," Emma said to her. "It enhances your extraordinary eyes."

Annabelle giggled."What is so funny?" Emma asked.

"Just today Marie was attempting call my eyes *exquisite*, but the word she mistook for exquisite I am not permitted to repeat in front of gentlemen. I can only assure you it was most comical."

Emma shook her head. "I wish I'd been there.

Her mistakes are often humorous." Emma then directed her attention at Mr. Woodruff. "I ask you, Mr. Woodruff, would you look at my cousin's eyes. Are they not the same colour as that dress?"

Spencer's gaze met hers, then lowered to the dress. "They are."

Annabelle was horrified. Emma was obviously playing matchmaker, pointing out Annabelle's best feature. Even more horrifying, Mr. Woodruff failed to praise said best feature. Men always remarked on the beauty of her eyes.

The first hand was played in a stifling silence. Luckily, she had a strong trump, so she and Spencer won. That bit of good fortune calmed her. She was powerless to keep from smiling at her handsome partner.When he smiled back, her heartbeat roared again. "Well done, Miss Lippincott."

She felt as if she had sprouted wings.By the time the next hand was dealt, she was playing with her old confidence. The others at the table were less stiff now, too. "You know, Mr. Woodruff, I am being most charitable to allow you to partner with Annabelle when I truly wanted her for my own partner," Emma said.

He eyed Annabelle. "I am most fortunate, indeed."

Now Annabelle was finally able to summon her voice. "It is I who is the fortunate one." *There*. That should make Adam happy. His houseguest was no longer being rude to his favored employee.

Spencer was now the one to avert his gaze. When his head bent, a lock of his rich copper-coloured hair spilled onto his forehead like a comma. She fought the urge to press her fingers to it. More than that, she tried to suppress the memory of being drawn into his embrace and feeling his lips on hers. She had thought that moment she'd first found herself in his arms the single most happy moment of her existence. Being with Spencer had made her feel complete. She had thought he was her past and future all in one desirable man she'd been foolish enough to believe in love with her.

"Mr. Woodruff," Emma said, "it sounds as if you're terribly attached to your sister's children."

His face brightened. "I am very much. This is the first time I've not spent Christmas with Lizzie and Hugh."

"How old are they?" Annabelle asked.

"Lizzie's seven--exactly one year older than her brother."

It wounded Annabelle to realize that had he not betrayed her, he and she could have children of their own now, children older than his niece and nephew. "Are you an indulgent uncle?" she asked, all the while wondering what kind of father he would have been. Had he not jilted her.

His eyes met hers. "As I will never have children of my own, I give them a great deal: love, time, and many special treats."

She sighed. "They are most fortunate."

"You heard Lady Fiona saying she and Emmie are putting together baskets for the cottagers," Emma said. "Would it not be fun if we could assist?"

Spencer nodded. "Nothing's more satisfying than helping unfortunate children."

"I agree," Adam said. "Lady Fiona's making dolls for the little girls. What can we do that lads would favor?"

A privileged, wealthy lady such as Lady Fiona

was making dolls? Emma had been right in her assessment of the kindliness of her titled sisters-in-law."My six-year-old nephew is exceedingly fond of the toy sword I made him out of scrap wood," Spencer said.

Adam tossed down his card. "A capital idea! We could make them in different sizes for lads of different sizes."

Emma was happily nodding. "And Annabelle and I could sand and polish them so the boys wouldn't hurt their hands on splinters."

"I should be happy to do so," Annabelle said, "though someone will have to show me how."

"My cousin has led a most idle life." Emma's eyes met hers, and she shrugged.

Annabelle eyed Emma good naturedly. "I cannot deny that I've always been pampered. I suppose it's normal when one's an only child."

Emma nodded. "An only child in a wealthy family."

"There is that." Annabelle could not meet Spencer's gaze. She was embarrassed over her wealth when Spencer had to work hard for everything he ever got. "All the more reason I want to assist in making swords for children less fortunate than I was." "Nick's planned sleigh rides for tomorrow, provided that the snow stays," Adam said. "We can get started on the swords afterward."

Emma nodded. "That's when Lady Fiona and Emmie will be working on their baskets. Won't this be fun!"

During the next hand, Emma chastised her husband. "I declare, dearest, you're not playing with your usual competitive zeal. I do hope you're not just trying to be charitable to Annabelle."

Adam looked at his wife. "Forgive me. Actually, I'm concerned about Verity. And Mama, too. They should have been here by now. I cannot help but to be worried. Since you'd never seen her before you wouldn't have noticed, but I thought Verity looked ill when we saw her during Nick's electioneering."

"I thought she was lovely," Emma said.Spencer nodded. "She's a beautiful version of Nick and Adam."

Annabelle was eager to see this Birmingham sister."And you must own, dearest," Emma said, "that Agar didn't seem to be worried about her, and it's massively obvious that he adores her."

"It's difficult to articulate, but she looked like only a shadow of her pre-breeding self," Adam said.

Emma patted his hand. "I'm so fortunate to have such a caring husband, but I beg that you not worry so much about Verity. If she'd been unwell, Lord Agar would never have allowed her to come see us when we went to Yorkshire."

Adam still looked gloomy. "I hope you're right."

"Chin up, old fellow," Spencer said. "I can take no satisfaction from beating one with diminished capabilities."

"Who said you're going to beat me?" Adam flashed him a crooked smile.

Adam did concentrate more the next hand and beat them, but Annabelle and Spencer came back to win the next round with strong hands.

Later, as she lay in her bed, snow softly falling outside her window and a wood fire crackling in her bedchamber's hearth, Spencer Woodruff dominated Annabelle's thoughts. How it had hurt her when he'd said he would never have children.

That had been his decision. Had he not treated her so cruelly, had he followed through with his commitment to her, he and she could have had children of their own by now.

What a pity, especially since he so obviously loved children.

It was even a greater pity that no matter how much he had hurt her, she was still in love with him. One part of her wished she had never come, never put herself through this torture of being so near him, yet another part of her longed for every moment in his presence.

* * *

At breakfast, he tried not to look at her. He kept reminding himself that he hated this woman. Yet her uncommon feminism lured him like a siren. How fetching she looked this morning in emerald green velvet. The delicacy of her hands as she buttered her toast brought to mind the many times he had savored the feel of those hands within his.He had once savored every moment he spent with her. Since seeing her last night, long-buried memories surfaced like corks on water, impossible to suppress. When on that long-ago April afternoon she'd indicated that she preferred him over all her other suitors, he'd felt as if his chest had expanded out of his waistcoat. He had been the happiest young man in the kingdom.

How had a penniless man such as he won the heart of a lovely young women from a noble family? The well-dowered Miss Annabelle Lippincott could easily have promised herself to many a man more worthy than him, men of family as well as fortune.No doubt, as soon as she had left London and returned to her mansion, she must have realized what a colossal blunder she had made by thinking of uniting herself to a man without means. He should have expected it, but every second in her presence had told him that they were *meant* to be together. From the moment they met, they had been drawn to each other as if by the pull of the tides.At breakfast, she had brusquely greeted him. "Good morning, Mr. Woodruff." There had been a time when his Christian name had tumbled almost erotically from her lips, when they were close enough for him to call her his *Anna.* He still thought of her as Anna.Breakfast was followed by sleigh rides over the newly fallen snow. The snow had stopped falling at dawn, and the day was crispy cool with blue skies overhead. To Spencer's consternation, Adam and his wife wished to share a sleigh for four with him and Miss Lippincott while Nick, his wife, and their young daughter shared a sleigh with William and Lady Sophia.Spencer would be forced to sit next to the woman who had ruined his chances for happiness. No matter how appealing she was, no matter how much he still desired her, he was determined to be as cruel to her as she'd been to him.He kept telling himself how much he loathed her. He had once been weakened by this woman. But no more.Out of respect for Adam, he would be polite to his wife's cousin while in his presence, but if he ever found himself alone with the she-devil he would wound her in any way he could.

As they stood beside the sleigh, he offered his hand to assist her in climbing in. She removed one gloved hand from her ermine muff, but before their hands touched she lost her footing while attempting to set a foot on the step. Her backside ended up in the snow.

He quickly scooped her up. She was a great deal heavier than she'd been when they'd known each other before. "Are you hurt?"

She looked mortified. "Only my pride. I am so embarrassed."

Emma rushed to her cousin. "Are you sure you weren't injured?"

"Yes, I'm sure. I don't know why I've become so clumsy. The wine last night, and now this."

"What about your dress?" Spencer asked. "Will you need to go back to the house?"

"Mr. Woodruff's speedy response to my awkwardness kept me from getting very wet."

"The rug will help to keep her warm," Adam said.

Once assured that she was unhurt, they all climbed into the carriage. He sat beside her, and Adam handed them a fur rug.It was far too intimate, but he couldn't offend Adam. He spread it over their laps. That intimacy along with her lavender scent affected him like an aphrodisiac. Their driver spurred on a pair of matched bays to bring them abreast of Nick's sleigh. A pretty little girl with ringlets of rich, dark brown hair sat beside Nick on her mother's lap.

"It's difficult to believe Lady Fiona is that lovely child's mother," Miss Lippincott commented. "I know the little girl looks a great deal like her father, but she seems not to have inherited anything from her mother."

Adam's eyes rounded. So did his wife's. They looked at one another--one of those conspiratorial gazes few others can decipher. Spencer *knew*. He'd known the Birminghams half of his two-and-thirty years.Adam cleared his throat and addressed Miss Lippincott. "It's not something we normally discuss, but since you're family . . . " He faltered.

"What my husband is trying to say is that Lady Fiona is not the child's mother," Emma said, "though the lady adores the child whom she refers to as *my daughter.*"

"I didn't realize Nicholas Birmingham was married before," Miss Lippincott said.

Adam's face was inscrutable. "He wasn't."

Miss Lippincott was silent for a moment. "I see. The lovely little girl is his *natural* child."

Adam nodded stiffly.

Spencer eyed Adam. "I've always held vast admiration for Nick. He would risk scorn in order to do what's right." It had always rankled Spencer that illegitimate children must pay for their parents' indiscretions."I'm proud of him, too," Adam said. "Fortunately, Society seems to have accepted him, though the only reason he cared to be accepted was for his wife's sake."

Miss Lippincott nodded. "How wonderful that the little girl has a loving family. Sadly, that is rarely the case. What a kindly woman Lady Fiona is."

Spencer had heard others disparage Lady Fiona's acceptance of the child. "What would the lady do when she had children of her own?" they had asked. "Surely the children wouldn't have to be raised with their father's by-blow!" Spencer almost praised Annabelle Lippincott's thinking, but he was resolved not to initiate any kindnesses with her. Not after what she had done to him.

What a dichotomy the woman was! How could one with such compassion have treated him so shabbily?

"Dear little Emmie may be the only child Lady

Fiona ever has. It's not my business to speak of it, but she has made no secret of her disappointment that she has failed to conceive." Emma now addressed her husband's most-valued employee. "I only speak of it in front of you, Mr. Woodruff, because you have been so close to the Birminghams for so long, we think of you as one of the family."

"That's very kind of you, Mrs. Birmingham," Spencer said. Even though he was as close to Adam as one to a brother, saying so would indicate an arrogant presumptuousness on his part, and Spencer was averse to adopting such a manner.

As they drove up and down along the slopes of the hilly landscape, Spencer watched Adam and his fairly new bride. Adam's arm around her, she snuggled against him. How good they were for each other. He'd never seen Adam so happy.The former Miss Hastings was nothing like what he'd pictured for Adam's wife. Spencer had always supposed that since Adam was possessed of such handsomeness and wealth, he would do as his brothers had done and marry a beautiful daughter of an earl. Miss Hastings was not as lovely as either Lady Fiona or Lady Sophia, but to Adam, she was the loveliest creature on earth.For quite some time Spencer had believed Adam's wife bereft of family and fortune. Little had he known that Sir Arthur Lippincott was her kinsman. Little had he realized all these months that she was a cousin to the woman who had trampled his heart.It had actually turned out that Miss Hastings--now Mrs. Adam Birmingham--had inherited a not insubstantial fortune from her deceased uncle, but having no need of it, she and

Adam were using the money to take care of London orphans.All of the Birminghams were good men. They deserved to be happy, and no one seemed happier than Adam.

Watching Adam and Emma made him melancholy. Were it not for the treachery of the woman beside him, he might have enjoyed such domestic felicity with the woman he loved. All he had now was a huge, gaping void in his life."I talked with Adam's steward, and he's got a workshop set up for us to construct the toy swords--or he will have by one this afternoon," William said.

"I thought perhaps that after Emma and I sand them smooth we might paint them," Annabelle said. "If we set them before a fire, they should dry by Christmas.""That would be jolly good," Adam said.

It was a bloody good idea, but Spencer wasn't about to commend Miss Lippincott."The steward said the workshop has some old containers of paint, but he wouldn't vouch for their usability."

"I expect Verity might have left some of her old oil paints here," Adam offered. "She used to always keep one set at Great Acres, one here, and one in London. She was mad for painting. Now I expect she's got another set at Windmere Abbey."

Emma giggled, but it was without her usual boisterousness. "I doubt she has much time to spend on painting now that she's so consumed with that babe of hers. Do you know, Annabelle, she has even chosen to nurse the babe herself?"

Miss Lippincott's cheeks grew scarlet. Discussing, even roundabout, a woman's breasts was not something normally done with a maiden in front of gentlemen. Even though Spencer thought she had to be seven-and-twenty, she was embarrassed to speak of nursing in front of him and Adam. "How singular," Miss Lippincott finally said.

Emma pressed her gloved hand on her husband's thigh and looked up into his face, smiling spectacularly. "If Adam and I are blessed with a child, I shall nurse it."

Miss Lippincott's cheeks turned even more red.

He found himself wondering if this lady beside him would ever marry. Would she ever have a babe? Would she hold her babe to a bare breast to suckle? The very contemplation of seeing her bare breast aroused him.

$\mathcal{C}$hapter 4

Nick's steward had thoughtfully provided aprons for the four of them--not that it was remotely possible Spencer could persuaded to wear one. A vise was secured to the long work bench facing a window. On the work table were two saws and two men's knives, all freshly sharpened and placed atop a stack of sandpaper. There were also two hammers and several jars of nails in varying sizes.

"Where's the wood?" Spencer asked.

"Remington said they keep pieces of scrap wood in old barrels." Adam went to a nearby barrel and nodded. "Here." He began rummaging through it, picking out the most suitable candidates for their project. Some were barely better than kindling wood, but many of the pieces were three or four feet in length. He put those on the table.Spencer joined him. "The smaller pieces at the bottom may be good for the hilts. Here, I'll get some." He set aside a dozen pieces shorter than a foot. "Does Lady Fiona have any idea of how many lads there are and what ages they might be?"

"I forgot to share that with you." Adam turned back to his wife. "Love, have you got that list?"Emma extracted a neatly folded list from her reticule. "There are eighteen lads, and she's written down their approximate ages." Emma placed the list on the work table. "You'll be able to gauge how long each needs to be by the lad's age.

Lady Fiona says she doesn't want any boy under four to have one because they're too young. So she's listed the four-year-olds and up to twelve."

Annabelle came closer. "Sad to say the lads of their class are considered men after the age of twelve while those of our class are still being educated at their parents' considerable expense."

Spencer glared at her. She must have known very well his parents had not the money to send him to Westminster, then to Cambridge. "I believe toiling in the field far easier than gaining mastery at Greek."

"Very true," Adam concurred with a chuckle. He then addressed his wife's cousin. "There *are* lads of our class who are sent to sea at twelve."

"I think it's shameful," Annabelle said. "And I abhor the practice of press gangs."

"You've hit on a topic upon which I agree." Spencer's gaze met hers and held for a few seconds. He looked away first, mad at himself for his physical reaction to her. She had the power to accelerate his heartbeat and deprive him of breath.   "While the men get their first sword made," Emma said, "let's see if we can investigate the paint's availability."

"I suppose we'll each make nine," Adam said. "Do you want the ones . . ." He squinted at the list. "The ones ages four, five, six, and seven?"

"Since I presume your wife will be sanding yours, it's not fair that Miss Lippincott get all the shorter ones." Spencer didn't approve of the way Annabelle Lippincott was being thrown at him. Adam and his wife must have thought they would be a good match. He inwardly groaned. He, too, had once thought so.And he'd thought Anna had too.

Adam shook his head good-naturedly. "You're always so devilishly logical, old Pythagoras. You want to take the even-numbered years, and I'll take the odd?"

"Sounds fair."

"Remington offered to have some of his staff make the swords for us," Adam said as he came up behind Spencer, "but I told him this was something we needed to do."

Spencer took his first slender scrap of hardwood and placed it in the vise. "Indeed." He cut the first one into two lengths of a foot and a half each for the youngest lads, then he sawed each into a point and removed them from the vise, freeing it for Adam's use.

Anna's lavender scent surrounded him. "Here, I can begin to sand one," she said. She had donned the apron and removed her gloves. He wouldn't allow himself to think about how lovely her hands were.

He stiffly handed one to her, then began to select a smaller piece for fashioning a hilt. Why in the devil did she have to stand so near? In spite of the way she intruded on his thoughts, he found a block of wood suitable for a hilt, took the knife, and began to whittle on it.

"I know you're a perfectionist," she said in a soft voice, "but I'd advise you to saw the hilts. It would take you entirely too long to carve out the *perfect* design you have in mind. They might not be finished until Christmas next year."

He spoke in a low, measured voice. "It's easy to see that you're an indulged only child used to ordering people about." His words had been calculated to hurt her, though not as savagely as she'd once hurt him. The pity of it was, every word she'd uttered was right. He *was* a perfectionist. It *would* take him hours to carve just one that would satisfy him. He *did* need to cut the hilts with a saw.

He'd forgotten that in a very brief amount of time she had come to know him better than anyone ever had.Or ever would.

He refused to look at her. He knew his words had stung. He'd intended for them to sting.

Her silence filled the cavernous building like ghostly aura. A moment later, she sniffed. He'd made her cry.

No matter how thoroughly she had trampled his heart, hurting her brought no pleasure.He was suddenly aware of how very cold it was. There was no fireplace here to keep them warm. Not that any amount of heat could ever thaw the iciness she had driven into his heart.

Over the next hour he and Adam sawed and nailed, and the two women sanded madly, smoothing the long blades.

Twice Adam frowned at him. He'd been careful to speak so low Adam could not have heard the cruel words he'd said to Adam's guest, but Adam was perceptive enough to know that Spencer was being rude to this woman.Finally, Spencer relented. "Do you know, Miss Lippincott, about your cousin's home for orphans?"

"My cousin has a home for orphans?"

Spencer nodded. "I believe she's setting it up with an inheritance from her uncle who was murdered."

"I had heard about her uncle's wretched death--he was related on Emma's father's side, so no relation to me--but I didn't know about the orphanage."

"It's only in the planning stages now. They've just found a property for it, and Mrs. Birmingham is busy working with architects to build a home large enough to house as many orphans as possible."

"I cannot think of a worthier project--and just the very thing I would expect of my sweet-natured cousin. I should like to help her in any way I can."

His back to her as he worked on a toy sword, he asked, "From Lower Barrington?"

She drew a long breath. "Emma has asked me to stay in London, to live with them. It's something I'm considering. Now that I know about the orphanage, there's a great appeal in knowing there may be something at which I could be useful."

He agreed. He, too, felt the need to help London's orphans. The plight of the city's hundreds, if not thousands, of orphans had always troubled him. Why in the devil was it that he and Anna always saw things in the exact same perspective?As he held a length of wood and sawed it, his hand was too close to the saw's blade. Before he could pull it back, the saw sliced into his index finger. "Blast it all," he hissed, jerking his bloody hand away.Annabelle did not hesitate. She sped to him, seized his hand, and wrapped the linen of her nearly floor-length apron around the gushing wound. "Allow me to press it tightly until the bleeding subsides."The others moved to them.

"It's nothing," Spencer said. "I just nicked my finger with the saw."

"Emma, can you cut some strips from your apron to bind Mr. Woodruff's cut finger?" Annabelle asked.

He could bloody well hold--and wrap--his own bloody finger, but he dare not speak harshly again to Miss Lippincott. He'd have her crying and Adam fuming.

It was bad enough that he looked so inept he could not saw a simple piece of wood, but now he looked as if he couldn't press his own finger. Worse yet was the close proximity to Anna. Her beautiful hands pressing his, her sweet scent, her very nearness all robbed him the ability to even think. He only felt. And it wasn't the stinging pain of sawing in his bleeding finger that he felt. With a potent hunger to draw her within his arms, he felt her presence. The sound of horses distracted him, and he peered from the window to see Lady Fiona driving her own curricle. A moment later she came into their workshop carrying a basket. "I've brought tea."

"We've had an injury," Emma declared. "Mr. Woodruff's sawed into his finger. We're going to wrap it now."

Lady Fiona shielded her eyes with a hand. "I cannot look, or I shall be sick. I've only brought some tea to help warm you. I hope it's still hot."

"That's very kind of you," Emma said. "It is rather beastly cold here, but we'll be finishing soon."

"If Woodruff would stop sawing himself," Adam added with a broad smile. Redirecting his attention to Lady Fiona, he asked, "Where've you been? It looks as if you've come from the direction of Great Acres."

The lady sighed. "I did. I was hoping your mother and the Agars had come. Nick's so worried about Verity."

"Are they here?" Adam asked hopefully.

Lady Fiona's brows lowered. "No.""I know they'll be here for Christmas Day," Emma said brightly.Adam's wife was jolly good about trying to cheer her husband. In this instance, it did little good. Adam looked dejected.

Lady Fiona did not stay but quickly took her leave. Spencer felt badly that his bloody hand had likely dispatched her.

Emma came to him with two strips of white fabric an inch wide."Be sure to shake off the wood particles from the sanding," Annabelle cautioned. "And make sure the back side of the linen--the clean side--faces his cut."

Spencer met Annabelle's gaze and rolled his eyes.

"Oh, dear, I'm being didactic again."

Emma laughed. "I am used to being ordered about by you, my dear cousin."

"I beg that you warn me to close my mouth when I'm in one of my commanding ways." She eyed Spencer almost apologetically. "I'm very sorry, and more than that, repentant."

He wasn't certain if she was talking to Mrs. Birmingham or to him.

Anna's pressure worked. The wound had stopped spewing blood. Once Mrs. Birmingham wrapped it, the four of them stopped for a cup of tea that was no longer hot.

* * *

Annabelle held the warm cup and in her hands and avoided Spencer's gaze. When he'd snapped such cruel words at her earlier, tears had sprung to her eyes. No one in her eight-and-twenty years had ever spoken to her in such a callous manner. The sensitive man she had once fallen in love with would never have hurt even the most insignificant insect. Yet he did not hesitate to hurt her.

What had she ever done to draw such hatred from him? What had occurred during the last eleven years to harden him so?As she thought of his meanness, she realized he was still the caring man she'd once known--to everyone except her.

His hateful words had been delivered for one reason. He wished to repel her. He most certainly had done that. The way she felt at present she wished she would never again have to speak to the man, never again have to endure his icy companionship. But because of her love of Emma and respect for Emma's husband, she must force herself to be civil to Spencer Woodruff. Adam thought very highly of him.After the tea, they returned to their work and finished the last four swords. The men then helped the ladies sand the last ones in the day's waning light."Did you find any paint that hadn't hardened?" Adam asked.

A disappointed look on her face, his wife shook her head.

Spencer shrugged. "If they can't be silver, they might as well look like wood. What lad wants a green sword?"They laughed.

For the walk back to the house they were forced to pair up. The snow had melted, and the sun had sunk almost completely behind the manor house. In front of Spencer and her, Emma and Adam walked arm in arm, chatting happily. She and Spencer said not a word. It was as if each of them were completely alone.

Chapter 5

Dinner was far too solemn. Even worse, Spencer once again found himself next to Annabelle. Her sensuous lavender scent infused him with a longing like he hadn't experienced in years. But he could not yearn for this woman who'd made it impossible for him to ever love again. He was determined to be strong against his weakness, his weakness for her.

The Birmingham men were obviously worried about their sister's delayed arrival. The always-joyous Emma Birmingham was determined to divert everyone's attention to happier matters. "We had a great deal of fun today fashioning the toy swords." She sighed. "Unfortunately, it's not looking as if we'll be able to paint them."

"You finished then?" Lady Fiona asked.Emma nodded. "Barely before we lost our daylight."

Their hostess nodded. "It was beastly cold."

Nick glared at his wife. "I didn't like you being out in the cold for so long. Why did you not tell me you were going to Great Acres?"

Her soft smile vanished. "I had hoped to return with happy news."

Emma steered the conversation away from worrisome topics again. "Tell me, Lady Fiona, did you and Emmie finish your baskets?"

"We did, and we're to deliver them tomorrow."

"Your little girl is so lovely--and so well behaved, too," Anna complimented.

Lady Fiona smiled, then met her husband's proud gaze. "We thank you. She has brought us much joy."

"Tomorrow I'll take her to *help* me get the Yule log," Nick said.

"First, she and I will deliver the baskets and the lads' swords, and then she will help me gather holly to adorn our house, dearest."

A smug smile on his face, Nick could not hide his deep affection for his daughter, though he spoke dryly. "The child won't be able to sleep tonight for her excitement."

Lady Fiona's sparkling eyes met her husband's. "She loves every minute spent with her Papa."

Little Emmie was an extraordinarily lovely child. Spencer had thought, years earlier, that he would enjoy having sons, but now he knew little girls were just as cherished. Seeing Nick and the way he loved that child made Spencer even more aware of the emptiness in his own life. Just thinking of his niece and nephew melted something inside him. And they weren't even his own. They already had a loving father and mother. How gratifying it must be to have children of one's own."You two are very blessed," Annabelle said in solemn voice.

Her words as well as her tone confirmed her regrets that she had no children, no husband. It was as if Anna had once again stolen his own thoughts. It had always been that way with them.More the pity.

Before he softened too much, he reminded himself it was her own fault she was childless."Indeed you are blessed," Emma added. Her looks conveyed so much. She and Adam must also want to become parents.Spencer inwardly sighed. He would have preferred staying home alone in London over being surrounded by three blissfully happy couples who reminded him how lonely and miserable was his own existence.

He shouldn't blame them for the way he felt in their company. Being with Anna accounted for his melancholy. He wished to God he'd never met her.

She had ruined him for anyone else.

Lady Fiona favored Anna with a smile. "Emma tells me she's trying to persuade you to make your home in London with her."

"Emma is too kind. It's a great deal to think about. My home has always been in Lower Barrington, but I have no siblings, no parents, just a distant cousin of my father's who's now the baronet and living in our ancestral home."

Emma nodded. "A fourth cousin we never knew."

"You still live with him?" Spencer asked Annabelle. It was the first personal query he'd put to her since he'd been shocked over seeing her the night before.

"Oh, no." She gave a feeble little laugh. "I'm the spinster in the dowager cottage." A blush hiked into her cheeks.

A blush on some women accentuated their ruddy complexions, but on Anna's milky skin it was lovely. "I would say a young woman like Miss Lippincott has a far greater chance of attracting a husband in London than in Lower Barrington," Adam said.

Spencer stiffened. "Some women are happy to remain unmarried." He almost said something about her formerly having been promised to another man but remembered he wasn't supposed to know anything about her past.

Before the conversation got too personal, cheerful Emma directed it elsewhere. "I am so happy, Mr. Woodruff, you've come to us for Christmas. I've been looking forward to the opportunity to get to know you better. Adam speaks of you so often."

"I do hope he's not cursing something I've done to displease him, for I do that a great deal."

Adam chuckled. "He's telling the truth. He's always reining me in when I'm taking too much risk with our clients' funds." He shook his head. "Spencer's always right. It was the same when we were at Cambridge. His understanding was so superior to the rest of the students, the faculty begged him to continue on. They wanted him stay there teaching the rest of his life."

"Fortunately for us," Nick said, "the Birmingham family's used to getting what we want. Adam made leaving academia most enticing for Woodruff, and we brothers could not be more well pleased that he's joined us."

"I lack for nothing," Spencer said, "for the first time in my life."

Anna's eyes met his. He'd forgotten how very blue they were. Like the deep blue of the Cornish seas. "I'm very happy for you."

"Nick refers to you as the fourth Birmingham brother." Lady Fiona bestowed a lovely smile upon him.He was not unaffected. His gaze moved to Nick. "You cannot know how much that means to me."

After the stuffed quail, meat pies were being passed around the table, Nick was pouring wine, and the diners were concentrating on their food. Spencer's thoughts were on Anna's words. Would she have married him then if he was as well-to-do as he was now? Would she change her opinion of him now that he was no longer poor?

Even though she was the only woman he'd ever wanted to unite himself with, he would not have her now. Especially if her view toward him had changed because his financial position had changed.

* * *

Once they had taken the same seats they'd sat in the previous night at the card table, Emma's gaze went from Spencer to Annabelle. "You two make a fine couple."

"At whist," her husband added.

Annabelle could feel the heat boring into her cheeks.

"It's nice, too, that you two are of a similar age, though I know it's not proper to ask a woman about her age," Emma said in her perpetually cheerful manner. "Being the same age gives you more in common to talk about."

"We've done little conversing," Spencer snapped, his gaze riveted to the stack of cards in the center of the table.

They'd done little conversing because he thought of her in much the same way he'd regard the rug upon the floor. He'd obviously wished she weren't there. He had completely ignored their previous acquaintance.Adam started to deal.

She eyed Spencer. "It's not I, sir, who's averse to conversing."

"Pray, Annabelle," Adam said, pausing in his dealing, "don't be offended by Woodruff's curt manner. That's just the way he is."

"Oh, I'm not offended. I've lost the ability to be upset by a man's disinterest." She could feel Spencer's eyes on her, but she would not look up, especially since she had just humiliated herself. Her spinsterhood had nothing to do with lack of offers and everything to do with the man sitting across the table from her.

"Forgive me if I sounded offensive," Spencer said.

She looked up and met his gaze. There was nothing contrite about it. Which completely changed her original polite response. "You're forgiven, Mr. Woodruff, not that I'd given a thought to your dismissal."

"If I seemed dismissive, it's because things from my past may have hardened me."

Was his childhood not happy? He'd always spoken highly of his parents and sisters. Was he ostracized at Cambridge because of his lack of fortune? Surely nothing that had happened in his successful adulthood could have made him so bitter. If anyone had the right to be bitter, it was she.

"Woodruff's just a confirmed bachelor who's been badly wounded by cupid's arrow,"Adam said.

Nothing Adam could have said could have wounded her more. She felt as if an arrow had shot straight through her heart. He had jilted her but had loved another woman so potently that he could never even be civil to another female. She found herself wondering what the other woman had looked like. She would, of course, have been beautiful. Annabelle could not understand how any woman could turn him down.

Nor could she understand why, after all these years, he still had the power to hurt her so. Why, after all these years, did she still love the man?

Adding to her humiliation were her cousin's not-even-remotely subtle attempts at matchmaking. She would have to talk to Emma in the morning. Did she not understand how embarrassing were Spencer's rejections?

She needed to get her mind off Spencer Woodruff. "Emma, your dress may be the loveliest I've ever seen." How pleased Annabelle was to see that her cousin who'd never been permitted to wear anything other than sprigged muslin was now undoubtedly one of the most well-dressed women in all of London. She wore a soft silken dress of pale green that was accented with ivory lace and richly embroidered flowers of the same ivory. She no longer looked like a girl straight from the school room. The low scoop to the bodice of her dress confirmed a hint of her womanly breasts. How self-conscious Annabelle was over the fullness of her own breasts which were barely contained within the bodice of her blush-coloured gown.Emma happily blew a kiss across the table to her husband, unable to suppress her happiness. "It's because of Adam I'm able to afford such lovely gowns."

Adam flashed an adoring look at his wife. "It's you, my love, who make all your gowns look beautiful."

Emma turned to Annabelle. "Am I not the most fortunate woman in the kingdom?" "Indeed you are, and you deserve every happiness."

"Is anyone going to play?" Spencer asked.

There was no joviality during their play. Spencer's brooding mood had cast a pall over everything. Each time she tossed down a card and looked up, his lichen eyes were upon hers, an inscrutable expression on his handsome face.She felt as if something was distracting him. Was he thinking about the woman who had broken his heart?Even though being in his presence had been bittersweet, she had craved being with him. But not tonight. Tonight she felt nothing but his contempt.

When their game was finished, she feigned sleepiness and fled to the sanctuary of her bedchamber.

* * *

Before Adam and his wife climbed the stairs, Spencer stopped in front of Adam. "I beg a word in private."

Adam's brows hiked. He nodded to his wife to go on, and he stayed in the drawing room with Spencer."I appreciate that you and Mrs. Birmingham think highly enough of me to play matchmaker with Miss Lippincott and me," Spencer began, his voice low, "but I beg that you not do so. I don't wish to be partners with her at whist, nor do I wish to ride in the sleigh with her, or any of the schemes you and your wife have concocted to keep us together. It's nothing against Miss Lippincott. It's something personal with me."

Adam's eyes widened, and he drew a deep breath. "Emma's disappointment will be nothing to Miss Lippincott's humiliation. Are you sure you wish to offend her like that?"

"I'm sure." Cruelty was to be met with cruelty.

$\mathcal{C}$hapter 6

When Annabelle returned to her room, a smug-looking Marie regarded her. "I believe mademoiselle is in love, no?"

Annabelle blew out an impatient breath. "Can I not keep anything from you?"

"It is just that after so long Marie knows you too well."

A fire had been laid, and Marie had laid her mistress's warm night gown on the tall tester bed where heavy velvet curtains had been closed around one side.

"And who is this man who has captivated you?" Marie began to unfasten the back of her mistress's dress.

Annabelle stepped out of it and the pantaloons, and her maid unfastened her stays. She had not told a single person about Spencer, but she'd never succeeded at withholding anything from her perceptive maid. She sighed. "You remember the man I wished to marry eleven years ago?" She braced herself for Marie's angry tirade against her former suitor.Marie froze. Her eyes narrowed. "You do not mean that horrid pitchfork!"

Annabelle could fully understand Marie wanting to stab the heartbreaker with a pitchfork, but to call him a pitchfork? Did she mean he was a devil? Then she realized what Marie had so clumsily tried to articulate. "You mean rake?"

The maid shrugged. "One garden instrument is

much the same as another to me, but that is not important. What is important is that this wicked man, he is trying to get his greedy hands on mademoiselle's fortune!" She began to slip the night gown over her mistress's shoulders.Shaking her head, Annabelle shimmied into the gown, moved to her dressing table, and collapsed onto her chair. "Nothing could be further from the truth. He thinks no more of me than a piece of furniture. He hasn't been at all civil to me."

Marie began removing the diamond pins from Annabelle's hair. "Mademoiselle is just being modiste."

"Modest."

"See, you admit it! Marie, she knows, that in the dresses you wore last night and tonight, you look most lovely. Men, they admire women with grand breasts, and yours are very grand."

Of course her boy-chested maid was using *grand* in the French sense. *Large*. There was nothing grand about those hideously large appendages to Annabelle's chest."He admires nothing about me."

Marie stopped brushing her mistress's hair. "That I do not believe. Did he not at one time confess that he was in love with you?"

Annabelle nodded.

"Did he not ask you to marry him?"

"He did, but he changed his mind."

"If he loved you once he cannot be, how do you say? Manured to you now?"

Immune. "I know what you're trying to say, but you're wrong. It's because another woman stole him away. He has admitted to my cousin's husband that the woman crushed his heart, and he can never love again."

Annabelle buried her face in her hands, weeping. Knowing that he had loved another woman that much hurt even worse than his jilting of her.Marie tenderly patted her then left the chamber as quietly as a kitten.

* * *

The following morning, Annabelle awakened when the parlor maid came to lay a new fire. She lay in her bed beneath the covers until the room warmed, then she donned a woolen wrapper and padded to her window.

Snow had fallen during the night, blanketing the parkland in front of Camden Hall and dusting the distant trees. Snow no longer fell from the gray skies. She stood there for several moments. Today was Christmas Eve. She recalled Nick's toast the first night when he'd hoped for the happiest Christmas ever. She prayed Verity was in good health and would make it to Camden for Christmas. For herself, there would be no more happy Christmases. Ever.

* * *

Spencer was strangely absent from the breakfast room that morning. Annabelle told herself she was far better off not having to endure his icy presence, but no amount of rational reasoning could lift her sagging spirits. The fact was she greatly looked forward to being with him even if he did treat her almost as if she were non-existent.Lady Fiona and Emmie entered the chamber, and Emmie could not control her excitement. "The lads loved their swords!"

Her mother nodded. "Emmie and I delivered them along with the baskets this morning."

Emmie nodded happily. "The lads all launched into sword fights with one another. It looked like ever so much fun." She spun to her mother. "Can I have one?"

Lady Fiona gave the girl a stern look. "May you?"

Emmie nodded contritely. "May I have a toy sword?"

"I don't think it's a lady-like pursuit. What do you think, Papa?" Lady Fiona eyed Nick.

His dark eyes flashing with mirth, he shook his head. "I'll not permit my little girl to have any kind of sword. And that's that."

"I'm sure your father will have something else you'll enjoy," Lady Fiona said. "He always does."

By the time they finished with breakfast, the sleighs had been brought around. They were to go to the wood to gather holly to decorate the house for the Yule.When Spencer came down the stairs Annabelle's pulse quickened. He offered a curt greeting to the group as a whole, avoiding eye contact with her.Once again, Nick and Lady Fiona, with their daughter, and William and Lady Sophia climbed into their sleigh.As Annabelle approached the other sleigh, Adam abruptly stepped forward to assist her. "My wife wishes to sit beside her cousin today."

The quizzing look Emma gave Adam did not escape Annabelle. The two ladies sat on the forward-looking side, and the gentlemen faced them.Something was wildly amiss. Had Spencer refused to sit by her? The man had the power to pile one humiliation after another upon her already overloaded shoulders. He hadn't even the decency to offer her a greeting.

No rug was offered today, either. Unlike the previous day, she managed to keep herself in an upright position. No plunging into the icy snow today. Was her clumsiness responsible for repulsing him? She had never been clumsy in her life, and now whenever she was with him, she embarrassed herself.

As she sat in the sleigh beside Emma, she tried to suppress the memory of sharing the rug with him just the previous day. Though nothing intimate had occurred, every moment beneath that fur had spoken to the potential for an intimacy unlike anything she had ever experienced.

Nausea rising, she willed herself not to cry. She somehow managed to level her voice. "We missed you at breakfast, Mr. Woodruff."

"I wasn't hungry."

"You might be pleased to know that Lady Fiona and Emmie delivered the swords this morning, and the lads loved them," Annabelle said.

Adam nodded. "They immediately began sword fighting with one another."

Spencer rolled his eyes. "Their parents won't thank us."

"We're fortunate, Mr. Woodruff, that you've joined us for gathering the holly," Emma said in her usual cheerful manner.

Annabelle turned to her cousin. "Emmie's the attraction for him."Adam looked at her. "Oh, yes! Woodruff did say being around her would help console for the absence of his niece and nephew."

"He does love children," Emma offered.

It was obvious they were all pressing too hard to carry on a conversation with this man whose manner was just short of being abrasive.

When they reached the wood, Annabelle was happy to remove herself from his presence. She was grievously unhappy that Spencer had the same idea. He moved away from her the moment they left the sleigh. All the married couples paired up, and she was forced to walk through the wood alone. Another humiliation. Was Spencer counting each of her humiliations as scores in some bizarre game?

Lady Fiona provided baskets and small scissors for each adult. Annabelle took hers and, because Spencer was staying near the child, went off by herself in the opposite direction. She lifted her skirts to keep them from sweeping the snow. Even though she'd worn her half boots over woolen stockings, her feet stung from iciness.Not a single holly bush was in her sight. Were they all on the north side where Nick and Fiona had led? The tall evergreens overhead blotted out the sky, and an eerie darkness and an even more eerie silence swallowed her. She was so far in she could neither see nor hear the others. What a fool she'd been to choose this direction.Just as she went to turn around, her feet plunged into uneven terrain, her ankle twisted, and she toppled face-first into the snow. Even though she was wearing her warmest dress--the green velvet with matching velvet cape--iciness seeped into every layer of her body. Pain stabbed into her ankle. She dug her hands into the snow to hoist herself up, but when she went to put weight on her right ankle, she gasped in pain. Once more she tried to stand but could not. She collapsed back to the frozen earth in defeat.

She sat there, legs spread in front of her, for several moments, listening intently for sounds from the others. Soon, one of them would come to look for her. Perhaps if she screamed, someone would hear her. The last thing she wanted was for the others to gawk at her latest mishap. It was bad enough that one of their party was bound to find her sprawled in the snow like an unfortunate creature afflicted with spasms. She'd rather it a single person than have the whole group stare at the pitiable, ungainly spinster she was turning into.What if they forgot her? What if she had to sit on the icy ground all night? She would perish. And it would all be Spencer Woodruff's fault. How long did it take before a person lying in the snow would die? It felt as if her limbs had already turned to icicles. Would she die before the sun went down? If the others forgot about her. . .

Eventually--it seemed like hours--Emma called her name.

"I'm here!" she answered.

"Where?" Emma's voice was closer.

"I need help getting up."

"Oh, dear! Allow me to fetch Adam!"

A moment later Emma and Adam were approaching her with mournful faces.As were Nick, William, and Spencer. She was mortified. What an oaf they must think her.Adam rushed toward her, but Spencer crossed in front of him. Without a word, he scooped her into his arms as if she weighed no more than a loaf of bread. She prayed she didn't break his back.

Emma's face crumpled with concern. "What happened?"

"I seem to have fallen into a hole and must have turned my ankle."

"She's freezing," Spencer snapped. "Anyone have a rug to wrap her in?"

Fiona started for her sleigh. "I'll get it."

Why couldn't it have been Adam who reached her first? She fiercely objected to this man knowing how heavy she was--though her heaviness was nothing compared to her total mortification. Never in her life had she been a clumsy person.Until now.

His raw strength, the firm set to his square jaw, the musky scent of him all rattled her. Try as she might, she could not be unaffected by him. No matter how wickedly he had treated her, he was the most appealing man she'd ever known.He set her in the sleigh and ordered her to turn away from the bench across and stretch her legs over the entire seat. Then he snatched the fur rug from Lady Fiona and spread it over Annabelle. "I'll walk back," he said gruffly. "You need to keep that ankle elevated to keep down the swelling."Without another word, he set off on foot toward the big house.

* * *

It was dark by the time Nick, Spencer and Emmie, returned with the Yule log. Spencer admired Nick for the way he allowed Emmie to think she had been helpful."Now can I help Mama decorate the house with holly?" the child asked excitedly.

"Yes you can, love. Your mother couldn't possibly do it without your assistance."

Spencer had foisted himself upon the father and daughter. He'd needed to remove himself as far as possible from Anna's presence. When he'd seen her lying in the snow, his heart had stopped. He'd been powerless to keep from lifting her into his arms. A warm mellowness washed over him as he strode with her burying her face in his chest. She felt so blasted good, so alluring in her glorious womanhood.He worried about her and hated himself for it.

From now until he left on Boxing Day, he vowed

to avoid Miss Annabelle Lippincott. Yet when they entered the drawing room and he saw her on the sofa, her leg elevated, an unexpected tenderness stole over him. Their eyes met."I really am bet-t-t-er," she said to him. "Lord Stephen had the very same injury at Eton, and he assures me that if I wr-wr-wrap it I shall be able to move about."Why the devil was Anna stuttering? She'd never, to his knowledge--and he'd once known her very well--stuttered when she spoke. Quite the contrary. She always spoke with the confidence of one who'd never been spared anything, whether it be the best tutors or the finest gowns.

"Wrapped it myself," the Stephen boasted.He touched Anna's leg? The thought of another man feeling beneath her skirts infuriated Spencer. Is that why he hadn't allowed Adam to lift her from the snow? Why did it matter to him who touched her? She was no longer anything to him. He loathed the woman.

"I do hope it didn't hurt your back to lift me," she continued.

"It did not hurt my back to lift you." He turned to Nick. "Need any more help with the Yule log?"

For years now Spencer had plotted how to get even with her for the hurt she'd caused him. He was reasonably certain his recent actions had wounded her. So why did he not feel victorious? Perhaps it was because rudeness and cruelty were in opposition to his inherent character.

That natural character had burst forth earlier that day when he'd seen her lying so helpless in the icy now. Even now he wanted to ask if she had thawed, if she needed anything, if her ankle hurt terribly. Being solicitous of others was his basic nature.

He didn't know whom to be maddest at--her or himself--for his recent deviant acts. He didn't like what he'd become. Because of her.

He helped Nick put the log in the hearth, and candles were lighted from it. All the females took a candle and a basket of holly and began to move about the chamber to adorn every window sill, mantle or table top with the slender green branches. *Woman's stuff.* Lord Stephen, who'd refused to accompany them gathering holly, had the right of it. These things were better left to the women.

Adam hung a kissing bough at each doorway off the main corridor.The drawing room was much darker than normal because the family custom was to use only the Yule log and the few candles lit from it for light.

When everyone was finished, they moved into the dinner room. Because it was Christmas Eve, Emmie was permitted to sit at the big table. Nick had her beside him, directly across from Miss Lippincott.Spencer was only vaguely aware of the host's small daughter. Most of his attention was riveted on the woman who would sit beside him. She refused to use a cane but was limping heavily. It was all he could do not to scoop her into his arms again and carry her to the table. Barring that, he fancied the notion of her leaning on him as she hobbled forth.He sighed inwardly. He was devilishly unsuccessful in his efforts to blot her from his thoughts. Nevertheless, he was determined to make himself immune to her. The first time he went to use his knife and fork, he winced.Annabelle's gaze swung to him, dropping to take in the newly wrapped white bandage around his index finger. "Your cut still hurts?"

"It does, but I'll manage."

She shook her head. "No. You must allow me to cut your beef." She reached for his cutlery.

His eyes narrowed. "You may be accustomed to always getting your way, Miss Lippincott, but I'm not some mindless child you can order around."

Her eyes instantly filled with tears, and to his mortification, she leapt from the table and hurried from the chamber.

As well as one could on a badly injured ankle.

He felt like a cur. Adam was apt to terminate his employment for his unpardonable rudeness. Worst of all, he felt as if he were bleeding inside. When she hurt, he hurt. And he'd hurt her most wickedly.

He bolted from his chair and raced after her. It was the decent thing to do.

She was almost under the library's kissing bough when he caught up with her. She turned and saw him. Tears moistened her face, and something in her eyes reminded him of a wounded animal. But she was no animal, she was a desirable woman.

She spun back and attempted to move more quickly. He caught up with her. Though she wasn't a small woman, she seemed small next to him. And fragile--like a wounded kitten. Her eyes smoldered. No one had ever looked more desirable.A primitive lust surged through him. He gripped each of her shoulders and gazed from her to the kissing bough. Then he pressed his body to hers, crushed her against him, and kissed her with a passion fueled by years of need.

$\mathscr{C}$hapter 7

When Spencer had grabbed Annabelle by her shoulders she'd thought he was going to shake her in anger, but a strangely tender expression softened his face. Before she could react, he crushed her into his arms for a hungry kiss. Her initial shock was quickly absorbed into the maelstrom that consumed them both.Her only kisses before--his sterile kisses of eleven years ago--had been nothing like this. Now his breathing came fast and hard as his tongue claimed hers. She should have been embarrassed over her own passionate response, but her mind was like one drugged with laudanum. Need trumped respectability. She clung to him as if her very existence depended on this raw intimacy.

He began to press a trail of nibbling kisses along her neck, then lower, closing his mouth over her breast. Shudders of pleasures lapped over her like a molten tide.Then as abruptly as he'd drawn her into his arms, he brusquely drew away and gazed at her with smoldering eyes. "I beg your forgiveness, Miss Lippincott. My actions both at dinner and here beneath the kissing bough are unpardonable."

Breathless and numbed by the pleasure he'd given her, she was trying to gather a reassuring response.

He did not give her the opportunity. He pivoted and speedily strode away.

For a very long time she stood there in the dark, trembling still as she stung from his most recent rejection. She could not return to the dinner table nor did she desire to confine herself to her lonely bedchamber on Christmas Eve.

She limped to her bedchamber to procure her heavy velvet cloak and ermine muff and ease her warmest boots and woolen stockings over her swollen ankle. Then she descended the steps, went through the entry corridor, silently opened the exterior door, and fled. Careful to keep close to the house on this frigid night, she trod through snow that came up over her boots.Velvety black skies darkened the landscape. Nothing more than twenty feet in the distance was visible. The cold wind stung her cheeks like icy needles. Each step crunched beneath her weight as she testily walked the perimeter of the huge structure and its pair of jutting wings. Only a single room was illuminated: the dining chamber where she'd so recently been humiliated. She paused beneath its bank of windows but wasn't tall enough to peer in. Nevertheless, she could picture each member of the Birmingham family sitting at their customary places.Would Adam and Emma be angry with her for running away? Had anyone heard the cruel words Spencer had said to her? They could hardly have ignored the manner in which she and Spencer had fled.   The Christmas Eve dinner would go on for another hour. The Birminghams deserved to have a happy Christmas with their loved ones free from woes. If she contributed to any melancholy on their part, she was most sincerely repentant.

As she stood there on that frigid night, she had never felt more of an outsider. How she wished she were a member of a large, loving family. How she wished things between her and Spencer hadn't gone so terribly wrong a decade earlier. What would her life have been like? Tears trickled down her stinging cheeks as she wondered if she and Spencer would by now have been sitting around a Christmas Eve dinner table surrounded by their own family and possibly his sisters and their families. Emptiness gnawed at her like acid.

She was vaguely aware of the increased soreness into her ankle. Lord Stephen had told her she should abstain from placing her weight on it. She gave a bitter laugh. Any physical pain was most lamentably overshadowed by the pain into her heart.

In spite of the cold, the memory of Spencer's scorching kiss warmed her. How could a man who was so logical that his schoolmates dubbed him Pythagoras be capable of such passion? How could a man who gave every indication of hating her be capable of even wanting to kiss her in such a manner? What a paradox the man was!How could a man who'd treated her cruelly have been so tender to her when her ankle twisted the previous day?

Unaware of what she was doing, she moved along, lost in her thoughts. As she rounded a corner, the howling wind whipped back her hood but she wasn't even aware of her surroundings. She was only aware of Spencer and the profound effect he had upon her. She realized now that all her recent acts of clumsiness were a result of the strong emotions he'd wrought in her.

Two more days she'd have in his presence, then she would likely never see him again. She could hardly stay on with Emma, knowing how close

Emma's husband was to this man who'd broken Annabelle's heart. It pained her to realize they would part on such antagonistic terms. Especially after what they had once been to one another.She became increasingly aware of the severe cold as she circled the house once more. That was enough. If she didn't go inside now they would find her frozen body on Christmas Day.With each step she climbed up the gilded staircase, she shed the ladylike shyness that had been instilled into her since she was a small girl. Until that torrid kiss tonight, she had never thrown restraint to the winds. But she had in Spencer's arms.

She wasn't even remotely remorseful for her wanton actions. Those moments in his embrace had been the most exciting in her life. Those moments reaffirmed her deep desire for this man, and only him. In her whole life she had never committed a brazen act.But she was about to.

* * *

What a weakling he'd been. All of Spencer's resolve to resist the creator of his unhappiness collapsed in the face of *her* unhappiness. He'd not been able to turn a blind eye to her suffering the previous day as she lay in the snow, nor was he able to ignore her hurt tonight. It shamed him now--especially after her eager response to his kisses--that he'd said such heinous things to her. For no matter how cruelly she'd once treated him, treating her in a similar manner brought no joy.He could not deny that when she hurt, he hurt. For in spite of everything, he was still in love with Anna.

The very memory of her passionate reaction to his kisses made his breath grow short. A woman interested in a fortune did not feign so potent a response to hungry kisses. Could it be that his Anna still harbored tender feelings for him?He fought against the urge to ask her, against laying bare his own anguished soul. Where Anna was concerned, he *was* a weakling. Efforts not to be clay in her delicate hands had colossally failed. A man had nothing if not his pride. He could never allow her to trample his heart again.Hang Adam if he was displeased with him. After the shattering kiss with Anna, he was incapable of returning to the others. He'd sought the sanctuary of his bedchamber.If he could only get through tomorrow, Christmas Day, with a semblance of his pride, he could depart the following day, sadder for losing Anna a second time, but perhaps with his pride intact.Just as he was about to throw off his jacket, a quiet tap sounded at his door.

Brows lowered, he crossed the patterned carpet and swung open the door.

There stood the woman he'd dreamed about for more than eleven years. "I must talk to you, my dear Spencer."

$\mathcal{C}$hapter 8

My dear Spencer? Dare he hope she could care for him in the same way he cared for her? He was nearly undone by her lavender scent as she stepped into his room.He blocked her progress. "I cannot permit you to enter my bedchamber."

She stopped. Her face fell.

"Pray, Miss Lippincott, it's not that I wouldn't welcome you here, but if you cannot be cognizant of your unblemished reputation, I must be." It was then that he noticed she was dressed for outdoors. Her cheeks reddened from the cold, and a dusting of snow covered the shoulders of her green cloak."You may leave your door open, sir. I've not come here for prurient purposes."

"I did not mean to imply that you were a woman of unguarded morals."

Her brows lifted. "Even after the way I kissed you?"

He could not believe they were actually talking about That Kiss. One simply did not discuss such actions. He blew out a breath. "Do not blame yourself for my ungentlemanly advances."

"I did not think them ungentlemanly. I found them rather manly. As you are."Had her voice grown huskier? Good Lord, could it be she was trying to tell him she had welcomed his advances?His bedchamber was certainly not the place for this conversation. He drew a deep breath, willing himself not to be seduced on this spot by a very alluring woman. "Have you been outdoors?"

"Of course I've been outdoors. Can you not tell from my clothing?"

"What could possibly compel you to go outdoors on a night like this?"

"I needed to think, and I think best whilst walking."

"Was it not bitterly cold?"

"Of course it was bitterly cold."

"That was an imbecilic thing to do. You could take lung fever and die."

She glared at him. "You should not say I'm an imbecile."

"I didn't say you were an imbecile. I said your actions were imbecilic. That's something altogether different."

"I did not come here to argue with you."

He raised his eyebrows.

"As you must know, it causes me great distress when you speak harshly to me. I have never done anything to warrant such treatment from you." She sighed. "I forgive you and wish to be your friend though I once wanted to be so much more than a friend."

He muttered an oath beneath his breath. "As did I, but *you* chose another over me. Did you jilt him, too?"

"What are you talking about?"

"I'm talking about the man you jilted *me* for!"

She put hand to hips and glared at him. "You, sir, are the only man I have ever wanted to marry!"

He could not have been more stunned had his departed father descended into this chamber. He could not be hearing her correctly. Had his wishful thoughts conjured her declaration? He was sure he had heard her father correctly when he'd delivered Spencer the heartbreaking intelligence that she'd had a change of heart and decided to wed another man.He suddenly realized that all these years he'd been falsely blaming Anna for destroying his happiness when it had actually been her father. That explained his own shock upon seeing her again and discovering she still bore her maiden name. Her father had obviously not thought Spencer either noble enough or wealthy enough to wed his only child."Oh, God, Anna." He moved to her, took her in his arms, yanked her into his chamber, and kicked shut the door. "What a fool I was!"

He savored the feel of her rounded body pressing against his, her arms encircling him. It was a moment before he could articulate to her the colossal lie that had deprived them both for long. Now the he was putting the pieces together-- especially her unrestrained response to his kiss-- he realized she still loved him as he still loved her. He'd never stopped loving her.

He finally drew away, gently clasping her shoulders and gazing into her flushed face. "When I asked your father for your hand, he told me you'd decided to marry someone else."

"Whatever can you be talking about? You never came to our home to speak to Papa. I waited and waited. Papa said you'd never contacted him!"

"I wrote to your father, requesting a meeting with him. He asked me to meet him at his club in London."

Her face collapsed. "And there he told you I was to wed . . ." She gasped. "My father had it in his mind I should marry that brewer, but I never considered Mr. Marsden." Her voice weakened. "Not when I loved you."

An incredible blend of tenderness and joy spread to his entire body. "Could you possibly change that to the present tense?"

"Change what to present tense?"

"Loved."

Their gazes locked. Her eyes filled with tears as she slowly nodded.

He crushed her against him for the second hungry kiss of the night. "I love you now more than I ever thought possible," he murmured.

He took her hand and walked to the settee near the fire. She sat. He didn't. "Since I have thoroughly compromised your reputation by inviting you into my bedchamber, I am eager to do the gallant thing." He dropped to his knee. "I am asking you to do me the great honor of becoming my wife."

Her face broke into a radiant smile. "I still recall every word you said that first time you offered for me at Vauxhall, still remember how happy I was that night. I'm even happier tonight."

"Is that an affirmative response?"

"Oh, yes!"

"Good. This kneeling is bloody uncomfortable."

He sat beside her and drew her close. He felt as if he could explode from sheer happiness. "Forgive me, my most precious love, for all the mean things I've said and done to you."

"I've already forgotten them."

"When should you like to marry?"

"As soon as possible."

"Good. This time next week, you'll be Mrs. Woodruff."

"I feel as if Nick Birmingham's toast has come

true."

He nodded. "This *has* become the happiest Christmas ever."

* * *

Later, when they heard the others mounting the stairs to their bedchambers, he took her hand in his, walked across his bedchamber, and opened the door.

Even though the corridor was in semi-darkness the brass sconces provided enough illumination for them to see the shocked expression on Emma's face."Adam," Spencer said to her husband, "I wanted you to be the first to offer Miss Lippincott and me felicitations."

Adam's eyes widened. "Felicitations?"

"Yes," Spencer said, a smug smile on his face. "My dear Anna has consented to become my wife."

Emma stepped forward and addressed Anna. "Are you certain, Annabelle, that you wish to marry Mr. Woodruff? You've only just met him."

"Actually," Anna said, "Spencer's the man who offered for me all those years ago."

Emma's eyes narrowed. "That awful man who broke your heart?"

Anna nodded. "He's not an awful man, and it wasn't his fault he broke my heart. Unbeknownst to me, Papa told him I was to wed Mr. Marsden, and Papa told me that Spencer never contacted him to ask for my hand."

"What a horrid thing for your father to do!" Emma looked thoroughly outraged.Tears sprang to Anna's eyes again. "Yes, it was."

"But all's well that ends well," Adam said cheerfully.

Nick stepped forward and offered his hand to Spencer. "My felicitations, old fellow."

Then William held out his hand. "Well done, Woodruff. May you both be very happy."

Lady Sophia appeared wildly happy. "I shall have my uncle grant you a special license immediately. You must marry here at Camden. What a wonderful Christmas it will be!"

It would be the perfect Christmas if Lady Agar arrived, but Spencer did not wish to bring up any worrisome topic--not when he was so incredibly happy.

* * *

Lady Fiona took her husband's hand as they strode down the corridor to their own chambers. A smile on her beautiful face, she fairly floated as if waltzing on clouds. Nick could not deny that Woodruff's joy was contagious. The man certainly deserved happiness. God knows he'd been more competent and more loyal than any employee the Birminghams had ever hired.When they reached his wife's chamber she launched herself upon him, needily embracing him. "Oh, my darling, I feel so blissfully happy and so beastly guilty for feeling this way when you're so worried about Verity."

He held her close. "Never feel guilty, my love, for being happy. It's what I want for you above everything." As worried as he'd been about his sister, he was equally worried about his wife. As the years of their marriage had ticked away without her conceiving, she'd become more and more melancholy. Even though he had greatly desired a son, he continuously tried to assure Fiona that he cared not if he ever sired a male. "I have Emmie, and I have you. I could not be happier."She was happier in these last few moments than he had seen her in two years. For it had been two Christmases ago--their first anniversary--that they had both pushed aside their pride and admitted to the deep love they held for each other. It had been, without a doubt, the happiest night of his life.

"I am also very happy for Woodruff," he said. "He deserves great felicity. I just hope Miss Lippincott can bring him the kind of happiness you've brought me."

"I am so happy for poor Miss Lippincott. I feared she was doomed to spinsterhood, but I do believe Mr. Woodruff is truly in love with her."

"From the way she looked at him, I believe she's besotted too."

Fiona sighed. "I have even stronger reasons for being so incredibly happy right now."

He stroked her silken hair. "What, my love?"

She inched away and settled gentle hands on either side of his face, peering at him with shimmering eyes. "I am now certain that I am with child. Our child."

He froze. He didn't know what he'd been expecting her to say, but it wasn't this. He'd resigned himself to the fact his beloved wife was barren. As the full context of her words sank in, an effervescence like an entire bottle of champagne exploded within him. It was a more profound joy than he'd ever experienced.He crushed her against him, then kissed her tenderly. "I do believe I'm as happy right now as Spencer Woodruff. Even more so."

She nestled her face into his chest. "I've been thinking about our Christmases together. The first, I will confess, I was most unhappy. I missed my own family, and I did not love you. Not then. The only nice memory I have of it was the lovely volume of Blake you presented me."

"And the second Christmas?" He knew that she'd felt the same explosive happiness that night as he'd felt."I've never been happier than I was that night when you caught me under the kissing bough after all those weeks I'd been deprived of your bed."

He did not want to remind her of the sadness she'd felt the previous Christmas when she'd cursed herself for being barren. "It's not that I don't adore Emmie and always will," she had said. "But I never dreamed we'd be married two whole years and still I would be unable to give you another babe. I am a failure." He'd lovingly assured her he didn't care if he had any legitimate children."Yet," she continued, "I believe I'm even happier tonight."

"As am I." He scooped her into his arms and carried her to bed. Their bed.

$\mathcal{C}$hapter 9

"Mademoiselle! I have been ever so worried about you."

Still wearing her green velvet, Annabelle strolled into her bedchamber early the following morning. "Forgive me, Marie, for alarming you, but as you can see I am blindingly, spectacularly well."

"Do not tell me that pitchfork has seduced you!"

In fact, he had. "That pitch-, er, rake who isn't a rake, will be my husband before the week is out, and I shall be Mrs. Woodruff." Just saying the name sent a bubbling sensation spiraling through her.

Marie's eyes narrowed. "One cannot believe promises made by men being . . . amorous."

"Your fault my judgment?"

Marie thought about this for a moment, then crossed the chamber and threw her arms around her mistress. "No. My mistress is possessed of excellent judgment. I wish you and your future husband every happiness. This man, he is most fortunate."

Annabelle danced around her bedchamber, shaking her head. "I am the fortunate one."

A smile finally brightened the maid's face. "Does mademoiselle wish to wear the red velvet to church this morning?"

"That will be wonderful. Everything's

wonderful."

Marie took the dress from the linen press. "Your Mr. Woodthing will love seeing this on you."

"Mr. Woodruff. *My Mr. Woodruff.*"

* * *

If only the Birmingham brothers could be as happy as she was this beautiful morning, Annabelle thought after the Christmas service as they were driving home in their sleigh beneath blue skies. Spencer put his arm around her, drawing her close to him. This is where she always wanted to be.

Spencer's eyes sparkled as he regarded her. "You look beautiful this morning, Anna."

"I do believe love must be blind, my dearest love. I do not deserve such happiness."

He kissed her cheek. "You deserve every happiness."

When she looked at Emma and Adam opposite, it saddened her to see Adam looking off into the wood, a look of distress on his face.

That the Birminghams' sister had not reached Camden Hall by Christmas was most upsetting. Any number of things could have prevented them from arriving, and none of them were good.At Camden Hall their Christmas supper awaited. They gathered around the table, and no one mentioned the three empty place settings that had been laid for Lord and Lady Agar and the Birminghams' mother. A servant lifted the salver to reveal the fat Christmas goose. Steam lifted away, filling the dinner room with the fowl's comforting aroma. She and Spencer clasped hands.

She felt guilty for being so blissfully happy when it was obvious the Birmingham brothers were worried about their mother and Lady Agar. Dishes were passed along the table and duly scooped into fine porcelain plates. Nick poured wine, and they all took glasses and awaited his toast.

From outdoors, the pounding of horse hooves echoed. Nick leapt from his chair and raced to the window. "They're here! It's Agar's coach." Then, as if he still feared something might have happened to his cherished sister, he eagerly watched. His brothers rushed to stand beside him. "Mama looks in good health," William said.

"And Verity!" Adam exclaimed. "She looks like her old self, does she not?"

"She does," Nick said. He turned back to his wife, and they shared a warm smile.

"I knew she was all right," Lady Fiona said. "Now what of my brother? Does he look healthy?"

"He does."

A moment later the chamber was filled with the newcomers. Verity--Lady Agar--did look like a lovely version of Nick or Adam. She was dressed to perfection in a beautifully sewn white velvet frock and held a babe who looked exceedingly well fed--and well loved.

"My dear husband has been worried sick about you," Lady Fiona said to Lady Agar as she embraced her.

Lady Agar turned to Nick, who had just hugged their mother, a stern-looking little woman who looked nothing like the dark members of the family. "You had reason to worry. Our coach got stranded in a Yorkshire snowstorm, but we were fortunate to be able to take shelter at an inn until the storm weakened."

Lord Agar looked adoringly at his lady. "My wife

was determined make it to Camden Hall for Christmas Day."

Nick gave her a big bear hug. "And so you did."

"Are you hungry?" Lady Fiona asked her elder brother.

"We are famished," Lord Agar said."We saved places at the Christmas table for you."

After everyone took their seats, Nick tapped at his wine glass with a fork. All eyes turned to the head of the table. His shimmering gaze flicked to his wife. "Fiona and I wish to share with our family our stupendous news."

The room grew so quiet, distant noises from the kitchen below could be heard.

"By this time next year we shall have a babe of our making," he said.

A flurry of felicitations filled the chamber.Nick lifted his wine glass, his loving gaze on his wife. "Let us all give thanks for this, the best Christmas ever."

It was, indeed, Annabelle's best Christmas ever. It was looking as if the second half of her life was to be as wonderful as the first. How could one person be so blessed?

She and Spencer tapped their glasses together.

"To us," he whispered.

The End

Dear Reader,

Thank you for reading *A Birmingham Family Christmas*. If you would like to keep up with my new releases and other writing news, you can subscribe to my occasional newsletter at www.cherylbolen.com.

Brazen Brides Series

If you have not read the other books in the *Brazen Brides* series, you might enjoy reading the first four installments which were full-length novels:

Counterfeit Countess (Book 1)

"Readers who like their Regencies spiced with danger and desire will love Bolen's humorous and sexy romance"—*Booklist*

How can Edward, the Earl of Warwick, get rid of the beautiful woman who comes barreling into his house with no less than fourteen trunks, a younger sister, a maid, and a very large cat? The imposter claims to be Lady Warwick.

Under orders from his superior at the Foreign Office, Edward can't get rid of her because her late husband held the clue to the identity of England's greatest traitor, a clue they must get. But how can Edward be with Maggie, the lovely counterfeit countess, day in and day out—and still keep his pledge to wed another?

His Golden Ring (Book 2)

Holt Medallion 2006, Best Historical Romance

"Who can resist a marriage of convenience between a couple who have nothing in common— but passion!"—Eloisa James, New York Times Bestselling author

The past year has been most unkind to Lady
Fiona Hollingsworth. First, the man she has been
promised to for half her life (Edward, Earl
Warwick, hero of Counterfeit Countess) broke her
heart by marrying another. Then her beloved
father died, leaving his financial affairs in
shambles. And now her eldest brother has been
abducted by Spanish outlaws who demand an
exorbitant ransom to ensure his safe return.
Desperate to save her brother, Fiona remembers a
chance meeting with the handsome Nicholas
Birmingham, the richest stockbroker in all of
England, a man shunned by her brother. She
casts her pride aside and goes to Nicholas, but all
she has to offer as collateral is . . . herself.

Oh What A (Wedding) Night (Book 3)

As Lady Sophia Beresford (recently Lady Finkel)
passes through the gates of her new bridegroom's
country estate and he begins to whisper in her ear
of the delights that await her in his bed, Lady
Sophia realizes she has made a most dreadful
mistake. There's only one thing to do. She must
bolt.

The bride-on-the-run is rescued by the
exceedingly handsome William Birmingham who
thinks she's a woman named Isadore, and though
he's the richest man in England, she mistakes
him for a common (but well-to-do) criminal. Since
she'd rather be dead than wed to Finkel, Sophia
pretends to be Isadore and take her chances with
the provocative Mr. Birmingham. But how could
she have known that her ruse would bring the

gallant Mr. Birmingham into such peril from the wicked man she married? And how could she have known her enigmatic rescuer would ignite passions she'd never known she possessed?

Miss Hastings' Excellent London Adventure (Book 4)

Having never left Upper Barrington in her twenty years, orphan Miss Emma Hastings is overjoyed when the uncle she's never met invites her to come live with him in London. Everything about living in the Capital lures her. She doesn't even mind sharing her seat in the mail coach with a gargantuan man whose belly rests on his lap. Even when her uncle fails to meet her at the posting inn in London, she's too exhilarated over the city's sights and sounds to be worried. After many hours pass and her uncle does not collect her, she determines to lug her trunk behind her as she struggles through London's streets at night to find her uncle's home.

Spurned by his mistress and vowing to never love again, Adam Birmingham, whose family is the richest in Britain, decides to get very drunk. As he's staggering home, he takes pity on a very small young lady who's lugging a very large trunk behind her. In the rain. Her destination is the home of his next-door neighbor, but no one answers the bell. Adam is compelled to ask the young woman to spend the night at his home. Promptly after showing her the chamber in which she'll sleep, Adam passes out on her chaise. It's not until the following morning he remembers that the lady's uncle has died.

When Adam learns that Emma cannot return to
Upper Barrington and that she has nowhere to go,
he offers marriage to the hysterical lady. His heart
is so shattered, he will never love again. Why not
make this helpless orphan happy? Soon after they
wed, they become convinced that someone has
forged her uncle's will--and likely murdered her
uncle. Their resolve to bring the murderer to
justice jeopardizes Emma's life. Knowing she's in
danger brings out Adam's protective instincts--
and something far deeper, something he'd thought
to never feel again. . .

Author's Biography

A former journalist and English teacher, Cheryl Bolen sold her first book to Harlequin Historical in 1997. That book, *A Duke Deceived*, was a finalist for the Holt Medallion for Best First Book, and it netted her the title Notable New Author. Since then she has published more than 20 books with Kensington/Zebra, Love Inspired Historical and was Montlake launch author for Kindle Serials. As an independent author, she has broken into the top 5 on the *New York Times* and top 20 on the *USA Today* bestseller lists.

Her 2005 book *One Golden Ring* won the Holt Medallion for Best Historical, and her 2011 gothic historical *My Lord Wicked* was awarded Best Historical in the International Digital Awards, the same year one of her Christmas novellas was chosen as Best Historical Novella by Hearts Through History. Her books have been finalists for other awards, including the Daphne du Maurier, and have been translated into eight languages.

She invites readers to www.CherylBolen.com, or her blog, www.cherylsregencyramblings.wordpress.co or Facebook at https://www.facebook.com/pages/Cheryl-Bolen-Books/146842652076424.

Lightning Source UK Ltd.
Milton Keynes UK
UKHW041809080319
338774UK00001B/28/P